BUTTER YOU UP

A GRUMPY SUNSHINE ROMANTIC COMEDY

FARM 2 FORKING
BOOK 2

LIZ ALDEN

CHAPTER 1
MOLLY

THE SIGN FOR THE CITY LIMITS FLASHES PAST LIKE A GREEN UFO in the dark—Welcome to Fork Lick. Population: 4,356. I'm not even on the highway, just a little two-lane road in upstate New York, far from my hometown in Washington.

I'm late—much later than I thought I would be. The sun had set long ago, and I had to pull over twice to let Ethel, the woman who was letting me park Vaniel on her property for the summer, know that I was running late.

Her messages back were concerning.

ETHEL

It's no trouble at all. These old bones keep me awake most nights, anyway.

I'll watch for your lights.

And please, dear, keep an eye out for Baabara. She likes to roam at night.

There are no context clues as to who Barbara is, but I'll keep an eye out for anyone "roaming" at night. A sleep-walker? Or is she Ethel's family? Friend? Partner? That's a weird typo, too. Why wouldn't the phone autocorrect to Barbara?

I toss the thought aside and shake my hands out from their death grip on the wheel. I've driven thousands of miles, but I still don't enjoy driving at night. Maybe it's trauma from encountering too many drunk drivers, or maybe it's me losing faith in Vaniel, my trusty ten-year-old Ram van.

He's not doing so hot right now, which is why I'm going to park at Bedd Fellows Farm for a while. I had to pause my quest to visit every lower forty-eight state when I realized my batteries would not make the trip.

Boondocking, legally parking my van for free in the wilderness, is my preferred way to spend the night, but I needed somewhere to stay with proper facilities. I found Bedd Fellows Farm on an app called Roots2Roam, which connects vanlifers with people who will let you park on their property. While some places you pay to stay, Ethel and I have arranged a deal: I'll be mooch-docking instead, meaning I get to park for free in exchange for working eight hours a day Saturday and Sunday on their strawberry farm. Plus, I get to use their facilities, and Ethel said I'll be parking right next to a full bathroom in their barn.

Finally, I see the Bedd Fellows Farm entrance. There's a wooden sign hanging off a post with a row of silhouetted barns above the farm name. There's a freshly painted matching addition hanging off the bottom that says, "Pick Your Own Strawberries."

As I turn up the driveway, I notice a big house off to the left with lights still on, casting shadows over the lawn—I assume that's where Ethel is. Suddenly, there's a sharp bend around a cluster of trees, and my headlights catch on a shape right in the middle of the road. I slam on my brakes before I hit it, causing a bunch of shit in the back to slam forward.

I hope to god that my laptop's okay.

A dust cloud catches in my headlights and gives the lump on the road a bit of an ethereal glow. The lump stares at me, jaw working and tail flicking.

A fucking sheep.

There's a goddamn sheep blocking the road.

A door slams. "Colleen!" A woman's voice calls out. "Baabara's blocking the driveway again!"

The shout has come from the house, and there's an older woman taking the steps down from the front door. She's pronounced the name with a bleating "baaa" at the beginning. Maybe Baabara wasn't a typo after all?

Beyond the few stairs, on the other side of the lawn, is what looks like a small building. I squint to make out what it is in the dark, but I can't tell. It's too big to be a doghouse. Maybe a shed? Or a child's playhouse?

By the time the woman is halfway to my van, the house's screen door opens again, and a younger woman about my age comes out. She's wrapping a bathrobe around her pajama-clad body and hustles to catch up with, I'm assuming, Ethel.

I eye Baabara, and debate the possibility of a guard sheep trained to attack strangers. Before I decide, Ethel and Colleen are at my door, and I roll Vaniel's window down. I'm sure I look like shit—it's late and I'm tired. I haven't had a proper shower in a few days, and my long, curly hair is up in a messy bun at the top of my head. My pale skin probably looks ghostly in the dark recesses of my van.

"You must be Molly," the elderly lady says. She introduces herself and her granddaughter, who's too busy staring at the sheep with her hands on her hips.

"I think I'm going to have to call Ethan," Colleen states.

Ethel makes a tsking noise while Colleen pulls her phone out of her pocket and steps away to make the call.

"How was your drive, dear?" Ethel asks.

"Good. Sorry I'm so late."

Ethel waves my apology away and smiles. "We're so glad to have you here. You're our first vanlifer!"

"I am?" That surprises me. Sure, there were no photos of vans or RVs on the site's pictures and no reviews, but Roots2Roam is kind of a new thing. I've been driving around for six months, and a lot of these places are still pretty old school, getting business by word of mouth or the forums.

"Well, I saw the TikTok videos, and we have so much space here, so I thought, why not? I sure did like the look of that lake you camped by in New Hampshire."

"Yeah, it was really pretty in the White Mountains. I miss it already." I miss the temperature, too. The rolled-down window lets cold air in, so I pull my jacket tighter around myself. Upstate New York's May weather is chillier than I was expecting.

Our attention is drawn past the hood of my van, where Colleen is simultaneously talking on the phone and trying to tug Baabara out of the road.

"Can you just—Well, I can't pick her up. You don't want Molly to drive her van over the lawn, do you? So put some pants on!" She grumbles and hangs up the phone, glaring at Baabara since she can't glare at this guy Ethan, I suspect.

"Have you ever met a sheep, dear?"

"No, I have not."

"Baabara's a merino—the finest wool you can get. She's practically my sixth grandchild. Ethan is going to come over here and complain that we spoil her, but my husband gave me Baabara, and well, maybe we spoil her a bit. After all, my Eugene did leave her some money in his will."

A sheep inheriting money? Wow.

My headlights catch movement, and a tall figure strides out of the shadows: presumably the mysterious Ethan. He squats with his knees, wrapping both his hands around the sheep, and lifts her straight up. She blinks, completely nonplussed, as Ethan carries her and deposits her...at the child's playhouse? What the hell?

Dusting off his hands, Ethan strides back into the darkness, shouting, "You're welcome" over his shoulder.

"Where is he off to in such a rush?" Ethel asks when Colleen rejoins us.

"I don't think you want to know, Gran."

"Ah," Ethel says with a knowing smile. She turns to me. "His ex-sweetie is back in town helping us out on the farm. Lovely woman."

"Gran, I'll show Molly where to go. Why don't you go back inside?" Colleen suggests.

"Fine, fine. Molly, I'll talk to you tomorrow." She pats Vaniel's doorframe and walks back up to the house.

"How far is it? You want a ride?" I gesture to the passenger seat.

"Sure."

I unlock the doors and Colleen climbs in beside me. She directs me to my parking spot right next to the equipment barn, points to the door to the bathroom, and wishes me a good night before climbing out of Vaniel and walking back to the house, leaving me to get settled in.

I turn off the engine and sit for a few minutes. It's not quiet; the sounds of early summer in upstate New York surround me, bugs chirping and leaves rustling. But I can't even see the big house from here, just the pole barn. After a few minutes, my headlights click off, and I'm alone in the dark.

Bedd Fellows Farm isn't quite what I envisioned. In our conversations, Ethel had made no mention of animals, talking instead about strawberries and soybeans and other crops, so encountering the sheep blockade was unexpected. Ethel seems nice, though, and Colleen might be someone I can befriend so it's less lonely out here in the boonies. Ethel, too, I suppose. One of my many skills is making friends, regardless of age. While driving Vaniel, I meet all kinds of people but don't hang around for long. I have to establish friendships quickly.

Finally, I get out of my seat. I flip on the single light above the kitchen and survey my home. I bought Vaniel from a couple in San Diego. Well, technically, I bought it off the woman after her partner had stomped off, declaring that van life sucked and he wouldn't drive another inch.

The van was perfect—exactly what I'd been looking for... except that it would have taken twenty-one hours to drive it back to Spokane. Dad insisted that I start my trip from San Diego instead of bringing Vaniel back home, so my dad—who was the whole reason I was doing this trip—has never even seen my van.

Now, I've got fifteen states left before I hit all forty-eight continental states. I'll hit those last fourteen states on my drive back home to Spokane, where my dad will finally get to see Vaniel in real life.

And then we'll drive down to Oregon, to hit that final, 48th state.

I almost quit. I told Dad I was going to sell the van and fly home. The flight would be expensive, but not as expensive as Vaniel's new batteries.

His electrical system, the one Vaniel came with when I bought him, has been limping along. I haven't been able to boil water for my tea unless I start my engine, and that's pretty bad. To top it off, I thought long and hard about it, and decided that the more expensive lithium batteries are the way to go–they last twice as long and increase my power storage. It's a better option for me in the long term, and it will improve the resale value when I decide to sell Vaniel.

I'm still hoping I can get this van back to Dad, and we can do some road trips of our own.

To upgrade, I have to swap out most of the electrical system, and that's beyond my DIY comfort level. Not only do I need to pay for the more expensive batteries, but I also need to find someone to perform the upgrade for me.

Hence, I've made plans to stop for the summer here. With

the free parking and work on the weekends, I can pick up another part-time job to earn some money and replenish my savings. Ethel even has a lead on a job for me.

The batteries can't wait any longer. I hope I can find a job in this small town.

CHAPTER 2
ALEX

IT'S FOUR-THIRTY IN THE MORNING, I HAVEN'T HAD ANY COFFEE yet, and my best friend is standing in my kitchen in his underwear, scratching his nuts.

"Pants," I tell him. I didn't think I had to have a pants-wearing rule in my house, but here we are.

Kit stops scratching his nuts, but it's just to stretch and give a great big yawn. "Dude, being a dairy farmer sucks ass," he says.

Kit is not a dairy farmer. He's my unemployed best friend who has crashed with me for the foreseeable future after quitting his desk job in Albany.

I'm the dairy farmer, and since the four-thirty wake-up call comes every day, I'm used to it. I don't own this farm, but my bosses, the Schumans, trust me with it. There are animals to milk and my crew to manage, and today, that also means managing this one, who's working for me in exchange for food and rent until he figures out what the fuck to do with his life.

Kit's hand wanders back toward his boxers, and I roll my eyes. "Pants."

"It's early," he whines, clearly disillusioned with the job even before his first day has started.

I smack his hand before it reaches its target. "Pants," I growl. My dog, Trixie, a miniature Australian shepherd, lifts her head from her food bowl and whines at my tone.

There's a sharp, indignant noise from him as he shoves my shoulder, and it is *so on*.

A few moments later, I've got him pinned on the floor, facedown, with a hand behind his back as he cries uncle. Kit never wins when he does this with me. Trixie hops around us, barking and bowing, wanting to be let in on playtime.

My brothers and I—and occasionally Colleen, my sister—wrestled a lot. I'm sure it was fun when we were young, but most of my memories of wrestling with my siblings involve my older brother Ethan, and they aren't happy ones.

So, when Kit tried to wrestle me for the first time during our freshman year of college, it ended with him hanging off of me like a monkey, and I was completely bewildered.

Eventually, I met Kit's family and saw how physical affection radiates from them, and it started to make sense.

And then, it was bashed into my head after repeatedly watching Kit wrestle with his siblings over the decade that I've known them.

Now, though, I hold a smidge longer and bring my mouth right up to Kit's ear. "Pants."

"Oh baby, talk dirty to me more." He grins.

I roll off him, and he teases me with a "bummer." Kit flirts with everyone: my gran, his neighbors, my cows…even once when he was drunk in college, a mannequin.

When he gets up, thankfully, Kit trots back toward my guest bedroom. By the time he emerges wearing jeans and a long-sleeve shirt, I've poured coffee into two Yetis and appropriately doctored them (black for me, sickly sweet for Kit).

We throw on our coats and head out the door four minutes later than usual for me. Two trucks are next to Kit's Altima, and my three key employees stand behind them, chatting in the crisp morning air. It's mid-May, and while it'll be comfortable during the day for outdoor work, the mornings are still chilly, especially this early. The sun is about half an hour from rising, casting a grayish hue with a touch of amber at the horizon. From here, we have a panoramic view of the farm I manage, Udderly Creamy. The house and the barn sit at the top of a hill, and the pasture extends down the rolling hills and out to the west.

Trixie peels off to do her business while Kit and I approach the group. Perry and Jesús are my two full-time farm hands, and Anna, Jesús's wife, works part-time for me. I have a handful of other part-timers, too, who do evening chores.

"Buenos dias," Anna greets me. She's a petite woman in her forties with graying dark hair and tanned skin. Anna comes every morning to prepare food for us. She and Jesús are originally from Mexico and have come here via the valley in Texas, so our meals are Tex-Mex cuisine you can't find in restaurants in upstate New York. Working on the farm burns a ton of calories and requires a lot of time in the morning, so we need someone else to run the kitchen for us. In a few hours, after Jesús runs the cows and goats through the robot, the four of us will be back inside for breakfast, and Anna will make lunch for later.

"Morning. How's Luis?" Their high school senior got his wisdom teeth removed yesterday.

"Tired and cranky. But he went through just fine, gracias a dios. Now besame."

She taps her cheek, and I buss a kiss on it. Jesús does the same, and Perry, the last of my full-time farmhands, starts walking toward the barn.

"But who is this?" Anna cries, spotting Kit.

"Christopher David Hutchinson, but you can call me Kit. May I?"

Anna's already in his arms, giggling as he plants a noisy air kiss on one side of her. She swats him away, laughing.

Kit follows me, calling over his shoulder, "I look forward to breakfast, Anna!"

I roll my eyes for what feels like the hundredth time this morning, and the sun isn't even up. But good news for me, bad news for Kit; it's time for him to shovel shit.

Fifteen minutes later, Jesús and Perry have moved the cows out of their stalls and into the robot barn for their milking, and Kit and I are shoveling the dirty bedding out. Trixie will spend all day running around as a self-appointed working dog; she doesn't have any official training, but she bounces back and forth from the herd, to the farm hands, to me. If something's going on in the farm, she likes to have her nose in it.

Since the temperature's nice and we're working hard, the barn doors and curtains are open, letting in a breeze. We're still in spring, but soon, as it warms up, this job will be a hot one. Everything gets busier in the summer. We have to keep the girls comfortable, so fans run inside the barn, and we switch out the water more regularly. Milking takes longer because they are producing more of it.

Right now, we only have to clean stalls twice, since they'll spend most of the day outdoors in the pasture.

I didn't give Kit much of a tour, but he's already marveling over what he can see. "A conveyor for shit," he'd said earlier in awe. "Never thought I'd see the day."

Now, though, he's shifted the topic on to something he finds much more interesting: my family.

"I can't believe Ethan's growing strawberries," he says. Ethan, my older brother, runs Bedd Fellows Farm, the legacy my grandad left him.

"I know. Grandad must be rolling in his grave." Well, Grandad left us with nearly a million dollars of debt on the family farm when he passed unexpectedly, so I don't feel too bad about that.

But there is a twinge in my heart whenever I think about

him. We didn't get along too well, and it'd been a while since I'd last seen him, even though our farms were just a few miles away. And now he's gone, so the reconciliation I'd always secretly hoped for would never happen.

"How do you feel about it?"

I shrug, but Kit doesn't let me get away with it. He scoops a big patty onto the belt and then stops, leaning against his shovel.

"I know you don't like to talk about feelings, but that's gotta hurt. You and Samuel always told him to diversify and now, all of a sudden, Ethan's on board?"

Samuel, my brother who's two years younger than me and the twin to Colleen, always pushed Grandad's buttons alongside me, but the difference was that Samuel was smart. He was always meant to get out of Fork Lick and do great things. He went to Cornell, for Christ's sake.

I, on the other hand, only ever wanted to be a farmer. Specifically, a farmer at Bedd Fellows Farm, but that clearly didn't work out since I'm here shoveling shit.

Guilt floods me with that thought, too. Sure, shoveling shit isn't glamorous, but I do love my job. As a teenager, I started working here at Udderly Creamy for the Schumans. They're the owners of this dairy farm, but they're retired and live in Florida. Between starting work at sixteen and now, at the age of thirty, the Schumans taught me everything I know about raising animals, put me through SUNY Morrisville, and slowly handed the reins over to me.

Kit's used to my silence, so he picks the shovel up and does what he does best: talking. "Well, I'm excited for the strawberries this weekend. Bedd Fellows strawberries. I bet they'll be tasty as hell. I wonder how long we can eat strawberries just plain until we get sick of them. Then we'll have to make strawberry rhubarb pie, strawberry shortcake, strawberry ice cream…ooh, can we make it with Udderly Creamy milk?"

And that's how my morning goes. I listen to Kit babble about strawberries (and then how ice cream is made, the soul-sucking office job he just quit, and his sister's new boyfriend) until it's time for breakfast.

I check my phone as I toe off my boots and step back into the house. Anna's made migas, one of my favorite dishes, and the smell of scrambled eggs and corn tortillas wafts over me. My stomach growls, but I'm distracted by a message from my brother.

ETHAN

Hey, you're going to come by this weekend for the grand opening, right?

Texts from my brother are rare, and not just because we don't talk much. He's terrible at technology, and even I, just a year younger than him, cringe when I watch him chicken-peck out a text.

This weekend marks the grand opening of strawberry picking season at Bedd Fellows. I've been spending more time at the farm than I have since I went to college, but it's out of necessity. When they need help, it's usually Colleen or Gran who asks me to come out. A few months ago, I went out to help plant the strawberry seedlings.

Even though I helped plant them myself, it's still unbeliev-able to me that Ethan turned part of the farm from soy to strawberries. I guess that's what happens when you get desperate.

As much as I don't enjoy spending time at the family farm, I don't want Gran and Ethan to lose it, either. While all five of us Bedd kids grew up on the farm, this has always been Gran's home and it's all Ethan's ever done. So, I better show up.

Sure, I text back, and put my phone away. At least I'll have Kit with me to act as a buffer.

CHAPTER 3
MOLLY

THIS MORNING, I'M EXCITED TO GET A BETTER LOOK AROUND THE farm in the daylight. I walk out to the bathroom in the pole barn. Once inside, I peel off my eczema gloves, wash off the residue on my hands from the medication using the special hand soap I brought, use the toilet, and wash my hands again. The bathroom is small and probably from the 90s: there's a solid wall blocking off the shower, which is the kind with a sliding glass door rimmed with faux-gold plating; the lighting fixture above the mirror has those huge frosted globe-style bulbs; and the white tile of the floor has seen better days.

But it's clean and sure as hell beats using the composting toilet in Vaniel.

After I'm done, I step out to wander the grounds.

Someone's out in the fields already, a man bending over and inspecting rows of crops. I know the farm is growing strawberries, which is why I'm here. Strawberry season kicks off this weekend, and I'll be pitching in by…doing something. I'm not sure what yet. Ethel just said that in exchange for parking on her property, I can help with the customers on Saturday and Sunday.

I do, however, need to find actual paying work, so that's on my to-do list.

Heading back up the driveway, it's a few minutes before I come around the bend in the road and see the big house. Through open windows, I catch the lingering smell of bacon and coffee, though it's quiet inside, and I'm guessing breakfast is over.

I continue around the house, and now that it's daylight, I can see the smaller structure clearly.

Ethel was right when she said they spoil Baabara. That's not a shed or a barn. In fact, it's a sheep palace.

There's an open archway serving as a doorway, and the tenant stands there staring at me while aggressively chewing hay. Paned glass windows flank either side, and in the left corner, there's a turret, also with paned glass, that extends past the shed's gabled roof and up into an octagonal structure. I've never seen anything like this.

"Good morning," Ethel's voice calls from the house. When I glance over, she's trying to push the screen door open while also holding something that seems to be pretty heavy.

"Here, I can help." I dart across the lawn to open the door for her. Upon closer inspection, she's carrying a cardboard box of jars filled with what looks like red jam.

Once we're both outside, Ethel smiles at me, open and friendly. In the daylight I can see better, and I would guess she's in her seventies. Her gray hair is pulled back in a no-nonsense bun, and she's dressed in sensible farm attire: jeans and a cotton button-up shirt with the sleeves rolled up. She smells like dirt and green already, and I wonder if she's been out in the field too. "How was your first night at Bedd Fellows?"

"Wonderful, thank you."

"Well, I hate to get right to shop talk, but you should get going. My grandson's farm stand opens at nine, and the sooner you get over there to interview, the better. And you can take these with you."

She passes me the flat of jars, and I take them with an oomph. It's heavier than I thought. Granny's got some biceps. I hold it while she closes the flaps on the top. It's a tight fit.

"Remind me, what's the job again?" All I know is that her grandson is hiring, and it's nearby, which meets my two most important criteria. I may be helping at Bedd Fellows on the weekends in exchange for keeping my van here, but I need an actual paying job during the week.

"Alex is looking for someone to run the farm shop during the week. Granted, he didn't tell me himself; I had to hear it through the grapevine." She clicks her tongue. "That boy never was much of a talker. But the Wallace kid wasn't working out too well. You know how small towns are; when kids have too much time on their hands and not enough structure, they get into trouble. But Frank Wallace only lasted three months."

She puts her hands on her hips. "Three months! It's not a hard job, dear. Udderly Creamy's milk and eggs sell themselves. You have to learn some of that new-fangled technology, but a smart girl like you will pick it up in no time."

"I've worked retail before too," I add. "I bet I've already used the POS."

Ethel gives me a sharp look. "Honey, I know what that stands for, and even if we deal with manure all day, I don't like that kind of language."

"Oh, no," I rush to add. "It stands for Point-of-Sale system. Not piece of...well, you know."

Ethel blinks at me for a minute and then throws back her head, laughing. "See, you'll be perfect for the job. And I'm sure you can handle my grandson, too. He's a little rough around the edges, being quiet and all. He seems to like animals better than people. But he is a good egg. And he sells good eggs." Ethel cackles at her own joke.

He likes animals better than people. I, on the other hand, love pets, but love people more. We used to have a dog named Bozo, but when I was in high school, Dad's mental health declined. He was struggling, and although he tried to at least *look* like he had his shit together for me, his inability to take care of the dog gave him away.

Looking back, it was the moment I became an Adult—capital A, Adult. Sixteen years old and deciding to rehome Bozo because my dad couldn't leave the trailer for his own health, never mind a dog's.

When I started my trip with Vaniel, I considered getting a dog, but it would live a lot longer than my road trip, and I wasn't sure what life was going to be like when I got back home. I'd already failed to take care of my dad and a dog once; it wasn't right to commit to an animal I couldn't keep.

Farm animals, though, I have no experience with, and my encounters with wild animals have been at a safe distance (with the exception of a copperhead snake that got into Vaniel in Texas. My scream was epic.)

I push the little niggling doubts away. If the job description includes too many animal responsibilities, or the boss is a rotten egg instead of a good one, I'll find something else.

It's a seven-point-two-mile bike ride to Udderly Creamy, which is a big plus for me. I have a bike that I mount on the back of Vaniel to use for quick trips, so I don't have to pick up my home any time I need to run errands. It's pleasant out today, and the weather's good, so it's enjoyable, even if I end up sweaty.

It's a farm. Surely, no one will care.

The dairy farm sprawls out over a hillside, pastures lined with wooden fences rolling out in front of me. I've stopped at the driveway, which leads to the barn and facilities up on the hilltop, but right in front of me, at the corner of the main road and the driveway, is the farm shop.

I almost prop my bike up on the fence but then decide that while the cows are way on the other side of the field right now, they won't stay there, so I change my mind and prop it up against the farm shop.

It promptly falls over because the jam jars on the back rack are too heavy. Thank god the jars are tight in their box. I take the jam box off and set it on the ground, then carefully balance the bike until it's somewhat stable against the wall.

When I walk in, the bell rings, and a man looks up from the computer at the counter. He's a few years older than me, maybe, with unruly brown hair and a wide smile. "Ah, my first customer," he says. "You've interrupted my game of solitaire." He winks.

"Actually, Ethel sent me about a job."

"Oooooh, and how is Ms. Ethel doing?"

"Um. Good? I don't know her very well."

The man stands up and comes around the counter. "Well, tell her Kit promises to come by soon and say hello. Now let's see if I can find Alex."

I follow Kit outside. He walks over to the nearby fence and puts his fists on his hips. He scans the pasture, which still has the cows in the far corner but no humans in sight. He puts two fingers to his mouth and whistles.

There's an answering bark from far away.

"Well, that should do it. Alex isn't very good about keeping his phone with him, so you gotta call Trixie."

"Trixie?"

Kit grins. "You'll see." He leans on the fence. "How do you know Ethel?"

I explain about Vaniel and my living situation. Kit grows more and more amazed, which is not uncommon when people learn I live in a van. But then he glances up and then lifts his chin toward something behind me.

There's a man striding down the driveway. He's wearing jeans and a flannel shirt, a seriously grim look on his face. He's got a full, dark beard, and beside him trots a dog, a miniature Australian shepherd without a docked tail.

When he gets close enough, he sends an inquiring glance to Kit, who puts a hand on my shoulder. "Alex. This is…what was your name?"

"Molly Perkins."

"Molly Perkins," he repeats. "She's here about the job. As much as I would prefer to stay inside and play solitaire all day, I figure you might be happier if I do some of the more fun stuff with you, like shoveling shit."

Now that Alex is close, I can see that he's a big guy. He has long legs and broad shoulders from tossing around hay bales all day. Do dairy farmers toss around hay bales? Probably not, but it's my fantasy, so I roll with it. He's also got that kind of rough-and-tumble cowboy vibe. They probably also don't have horses here, but this is just another improbable extension of the fantasy.

Um, I like it. The man who is going to interview me for the job is a stone-cold hottie. Just my luck.

Alex nods politely, opens the door with precise movements, and steps inside, holding it open for me. The dog follows him in.

I bend down, picking up the jam jars and hoisting them against my chest. Kit is still leaning on the fence, his attention on his phone now that he has handed me over to Alex. Stepping inside, I take a better look around this time.

It's kinda…disappointing. I was hoping for something like Rose Apothecary but it's more 1990s closet with white-coated wire racks and a few stand-up fridges. Alex strides over to the counter, his boots leaving behind faint prints on the sealed cement floor. His dog settles into a dog bed in the corner. Alex stands at the computer, back ramrod straight, twines his hands together on the counter, and asks, "Do you have a resume?"

I almost respond, "Sir, yes, sir." He has the posture of someone who was in the military and doesn't know he's gotten out. Instead, I heft the box of jam on the counter. "First, these are for you."

"Thank you, but we aren't in the habit of trading or selling products manufactured by strangers."

"Oh, no, these are from Ethel."

The man looks down at the jams. Back up at me. Back down at the jams.

"These jams? My gran made them?"

"Yes. You didn't know she made jams?"

"No."

I cast about for anything else to say and come up with a big fat zero, which is unusual for me.

"What am I supposed to do with all these jams?"

"Sell them, I think? This is a farm stand, right? Or eat them?"

"Hm," is all he says.

"And, uh, the job?"

"Yes." Alex ducks down, shuffling under the counter, and pulls out some papers. "The job is managing this farm stand. You have to be good with customers, our point of sales system, and basic arithmetic."

"Check, check, and check." I grin at him.

"Do you have a resume?" he asks again.

This time, I pull it out of my backpack, and he reads it over before asking me a few very brief yes or no questions. Then he asks, "Have you ever worked on a farm before?"

"Not a real one."

Alex stares at me for a moment. "What do you mean 'a real one'?" His eyebrow moves a hair north, which I take as a sign that he's intrigued.

"I play Stardew Valley. Have you heard of it?"

He blinks.

"It's this retro computer game where you inherit a farm, grow crops, raise animals, and basically dominate the small town until you amass enormous wealth. You can raise cows, goats, sheep, and pigs, but you've got to feed, pet, and milk them every day."

"You milk...digital cows?" The eyebrow has crept up farther, which fills me with a perverse sense of excitement.

"Yeah, I mean, just like real life, they have to be milked, or they get angry."

"Angry," he echoes. It doesn't sound like a question.

"Yeah, they get these little angry clouds over their heads. So I could be a Stardew Valley farmer for real here, with the cows, I guess. You don't have any sheep, goats, or pigs, do you? Oh wait, I've already met Baabara, so I've got the sheep covered."

"We have goats," he corrects me. "You realize you won't actually be milking any cows, right?"

"Don't take away my dreams," I joke. I have never once dreamed about milking cows, vastly preferring to take care of virtual ones.

Alex's eyebrow goes down. Ah, well.

He gives me a brief tutorial on the POS system, which isn't one I've used before, but they all typically translate pretty well. I ring him up on a fake order and show off my chops by trying to upsell him butter and cheese.

"We don't sell butter and cheese," he grumbles.

Looking around, it's pretty slim pickings. There's milk— the bright colored labels differentiating between types like whole and skim—eggs, and some farm merch, like sweatshirts and T-shirts.

"Who are your customers?" I ask.

"We run a CSA program that covers the region from Poughkeepsie to Albany. We do some bulk orders for local restaurants and shops, and we have a few city folks who pass by on their drives upstate and stop in to buy local products. A bit of local traffic. Some homesteaders that haven't made the jump to large animals yet. But most of our milk goes to a dairy cooperative."

I hum, and Alex asks if I have any other questions.

No, no, I don't. It's not exactly the bustling gift shop, small bookstore, or artsy stationery store that I've worked for in the past—all of which were seasonal tourist-dependent jobs—but they need someone. I need a job, and Ethel seems pretty set on me working here.

"I'll call you," Alex says without a smile, offering me his hand for a shake. "Pleasure meeting you."

I respond with my own niceties and turn to walk out. Just before I get out the door, I pause and glance back over my shoulder. Alex's eyes quickly dart up from a part of my anatomy decidedly lower than my head, and I swear for a minute his cheeks pinken. I think he was just checking out my ass. I tamp down inappropriate belly flutters for my boss. "Can I say hi to your puppy?"

He looks at his dog. "Trixie, say hello."

Trixie gets up off the floor, tail wagging the dog at fifty miles per hour, but she keeps a respectful distance and then sits. She offers a paw like a prim and proper lady, despite the floor behind her ass getting a good sweeping. "Hello, Trixie." I say, shaking her hand and glancing back at Alex.

"Good girl," he says, and I know he's talking to the dog, but damn. That's hot. "Okay."

"Okay" must be her version of "go wild." Trixie gets up again, butt wagging everywhere, and gives me a good and proper sniff when I offer the back of my hand. She does not jump, though she's clearly thought about it and then thought the better of it.

"That's enough. Goodbye, Molly."

And I'm dismissed. Ethel wasn't kidding about Alex not being a talker.

I need the money, though, and I'll be working by myself in the farm stand. No animal encounters necessary, and minimal contact with my boss, who says he has an office in the barn up the hill.

It'll be totally worth it to get Vaniel back up and running again.

CHAPTER 4
ALEX

MOLLY LEAVES THE SHOP AND BRIEFLY SPEAKS TO KIT BEFORE climbing on her bike and peddling off. I pretend to be busy with paperwork instead of trying to listen to their conversation, but the hum of the surrounding refrigerators is too loud to catch anything. Kit saunters in and grins at me.

"Does she have the job?"

I hold up her resume. "I have to call her references, but probably."

He fist pumps. "Yes. Put me back in the barn, buddy."

I give him an eyebrow raise and step out from the counter to let him back in. He settles back in at the computer and minimizes the POS software, revealing a game of Solitaire. Instead of playing, though, he leans forward, his elbows on the counter.

"You should ask her out."

I choke on air.

"What?"

"She's cute as hell, and she's into you."

Well, I can't argue the first one. Molly has long, curly red hair that bounces when she moves, which she does frequently. Even just standing and talking to me, she was moving around, rocking on her feet. Molly had to look up at me, which almost everyone does since I'm so tall, but she's pretty short—maybe a foot shorter than me. Her features were delicate, with high cheekbones and freckles. Very pretty.

"Do you have an HR department? Cause you're gonna need one for this."

"I'm the HR department."

"Conflict of interest," he claims. "I'm your new HR department."

I cross my arms over my chest. "Are you gonna call her references?"

"Making phone calls? Ew, no."

I give him a glare.

"No, wait! Make me her boss. We might have to form a subsidiary corporation and a shell company to move things around so that you're not her boss's boss." Kit moves his hands around like a street performer taking bets on which cup the ball is under.

"You don't have any idea what those things are, do you?"

"Nope, but I'm just trying to help my best friend ask his soulmate out."

Sure, when pigs fly. Kit is the sole reason I've had relationships with women. He would drag me to trivia night or happy hour. I'm not very good at talking to women, but he is. Once he breaks the ice, it's easier for me to have a conversation.

It's been a crutch over the years, I know. And I have gotten better about striking out on my own. I've even had a couple of flings with tourists passing through Climax, the bigger town about half an hour away and closer to the highway.

When you visit a town like Climax, making jokes about the name really gets the ball rolling.

Don't even get me started on soul mates, though. Kit is a hopeless romantic, and by that I mean he falls in love every day and twice on Sundays.

"What makes you think I even like her?" I grumble.

Kit says nothing. He just lifts a finger to my forehead and circles my eyebrows. Kit swears my eyebrows are the most expressive part of me.

He might have a point.

"While she was busy checking out all of this," His finger now circles my whole body. "I was watching all of this." It zones in again on my eyebrows.

I decide it's best to ignore this and pat my jeans pockets, looking for my phone.

Kit rolls his eyes. "It's up in your office, I'm sure."

"Anything important enough is happening on the farm," I grumble, my usual reason for leaving my phone at my desk. That and I work with the bodily fluids of farm animals all day. Besides, most of my notifications are from our social media accounts, and it's just a reminder of yet another thing I've put on the back burner...mostly because I just really fucking hate social media. Any time I try to post something, my captions just sound inane. No one wants to hear about the nitty gritty aspects of dairy farm work, which is what I'm up to my elbows in every day.

"Fine, go do the boring, responsible thing and hire Molly." He rubs his hands together like a villain. "Time for solitaire."

I pick up Molly's resume, folding it in half and tucking it into my back pocket. On the way out, I tap my leg and Trixie jumps back up from her dog bed and follows me out.

When I get to my office, I pick up my phone and dial the first reference.

I chat with a pleasant woman who reminds me of my gran. She owned a stationery store Molly worked at for four months, and when I ask why Molly left, the lady tells me she had to shut down the store. "A Hallmark opened up around the corner, and I couldn't compete. Plus, my son suggested I move down to California, and I was tired of the winters."

Next, a guy answers, and I explain who I am and what the

job is and ask him about Molly's employment at his bookstore. "She was an exceptional employee," he says. "Real passionate about books. Where did you say you were again?"

"Fork Lick, New York."

There's a pause. I'm not sure if that's all he needed to know, so after a beat, I ask him why Molly left.

He hesitates, and that worries me. "She had some personal trouble. Had to turn in her notice. Did she mention her father?"

"No, sir."

There's a sigh on the other end of the line. "I guess I better call him and make sure he's okay."

"Is there anything that would affect Molly's ability to work?"

"No, no. She'll do great with customers. I'd hire her again."

I ask him a few more questions and then say goodbye.

The last reference is Molly's current job, which she says she does part-time from the van. A woman answers, and everything I ask her checks out—Molly works about four hours a week creating social media content for her van life blog. She is a reliable employee, creative, yada yada.

After we hang up, I lean back in my chair. I'm going to hire Molly, but Kit got in my head, making me think about *liking* her.

Probably for the best, anyway. Molly's living at my family's farm, working for both of us and out of here in three months. Plus, she's high energy, babbling on and bouncing while she talks.

Perfect for a customer service job. Not for me.

I email her a job offer and, with a shake of my head, leave my office heading for the calf hutches.

Soul mates.

As if I could be soul mates with someone who milks virtual cows, for fuck's sake.

CHAPTER 5
ALEX

THE MORNING OF THE STRAWBERRY GRAND OPENING, I SWING BY after the milking to drop off a few crates of strawberry-flavored milk. While I heft the cases of pink liquid, Trixie begins her favorite pastime on the farm—watching Baabara, which, in this case, means trotting around and sniffing Baabara's house to see if any invaders have dared set foot in the area. Eventually, she'll settle down to watch the sheep munch on the hay bale that I'm sure my brother just put in to keep Baabara entertained and happy while guests are running around the property.

We don't normally make flavored milk, and I was loudly against the idea, but Gran put her foot down and insisted that this was a family event, so we had to have Udderly Creamy milk, and it *had* to be strawberry flavored.

Gran made the strawberry syrup herself with the early strawberries and brought it over for the bottling.

We're not the only vendor here. My brother invited a few local crafters and food purveyors, and the smells that waft through the farm mingle: baked goods and lavender soaps.

I look for Molly, but everything is pretty hectic, with getting the booths set up and vendors ready to go. When I do see her, she's running around with a clipboard and directing people, tilting her papers this way and that to read the map and flipping through pages, her pale brow wrinkled in concentration.

Kit was wrong, damn it. She's not cute. She's sexy as hell. With her hair pulled up in a bun and tendrils framing her face, her pink lips dimpling under her teeth as she concentrates, she looks like she fits right in here.

She's wearing white shorts and a jean jacket over a T-shirt —it's chillier than it was yesterday, but still sunny. My gaze travels down her legs, which were clad in khaki pants for the interview and are on display now.

I blink. Ugh. Where's my HR department? Oh, right, back at the farm. I scowl at myself and look away before Molly can catch me being creepy.

I feel different eyes on me, though, and turn my head to find my brother, Ethan, climbing down a ladder and heading my way.

"I owe you a phone call. We should talk," is his opener.

I heave a sigh, hands in my pockets. I've heard this story before. A few months ago, in fact, and nothing came of it. "Sure."

Ethan catches the doubts in my tone. "What is that supposed to mean?"

I shrug and bite the side of my tongue. "It's been months since you said that."

Ethan gestures around. "Well, we've got shit going on right now."

I look away, and we're both quiet for a moment. I don't think my brother, the golden child and Grandad's favorite, understands what it's like to get your hopes up for scraps of attention, only to be let down once again.

My eyes fall on Lia. Maybe Ethan does get it but in a different way. Here's his high school sweetheart, who disappeared for a decade, back in town and looking mighty happy.

And the way Ethan looks at her…

"She's staying, then?" I stick my thumb out in Lia's direction. Ethan's face lights up like I haven't seen since we were kids. "Good. Always thought you two were good together."

Molly walks toward us, and I straighten up. She taps her clipboard and says to my brother, "We are as ready as we'll ever be, boss."

"I told you not to call me that. I think Lia's the one really in charge. Or maybe Gran since she's the one who hired you."

She shakes her head. "Well, if we're going by who is actually paying me…" Molly grins at me and pokes at the Udderly Creamy Farm polo I'm wearing. I subtly flex the muscle beneath her finger. Lord, help me. "Boss," she says with a lilting tease.

That's my cue to get out of here—when I start acting like an idiot—so I make my excuses and leave. Trixie trots out from Baabara's house, and we head back to the farm and get to work.

In the late afternoon, my sister texts me that things are winding down and I should come back to see how it went. When I pull up and open the door, Trixie vaults out and starts the same thing she did this morning—sniffing around Baabara's enclosure. This time is much more frenetic, and I'm going to guess Baabara had a lot of visitors today.

There are still a few customers lingering around, paying for their haul.

If I had any doubt that Molly was great with customers, it is washed away watching her at Bedd Fellows Farm selling strawberries. She's not even selling the fruit, really; she's selling the experience. She's giving kids stickers and animatedly exclaiming every time she weighs a bucket as if she's never seen such a giant mound of strawberries. The kids eat it up, and the parents leave happy.

Molly starts working for me on Thursday. I would have had her sooner, but Molly said she needed a few days to settle in. That was okay because I've had Kit around, but he's eager to move back to the barn. He's there now, working with Zach, my evening manager, bedding my herd down for the night, and I'm here to see how the day went.

Bedd Fellows Farm is like I've never seen it. There are red balloons everywhere, tables set up with home goods like soap and candles, and a bakery display.

I guess I was wrong about the milk because the abomination is pretty dang popular. The Igloo that kept the bottles chilled is empty.

I linger, chatting with the couple that owns the Feed 'n Seed, Diego and Chen, until they leave. I find my brother counting receipts and Molly counting the money in her cash box.

The family crowds in, Gran pouring tea for us, the twins—Colleen and Sam—talking to each other, Lia opening her laptop to crunch numbers.

Finally, she looks up, and my brother rushes to her side. A twitch of envy hits me, seeing how much he wants to be near her, how he hangs onto her every word and looks at her like she hung the moon.

My eyes shift to Molly and she's staring right at me. I fix my face so I don't look sappy by frowning.

"Today was incredible, Ethan. We made so much more revenue than we hoped."

Ethan sags in relief, and the rest of us get closer, eager for details.

But Lia doesn't look as happy as I would expect. "We always knew it wasn't going to be enough, though. You're still in a really precarious place."

I frown. Of course, I didn't think strawberries were gonna fix everything, but it's an entire season of sales, and it should only improve as the different varieties fill in and word spreads about the farm. But I bite my tongue. Lia knows all this, and so does Ethan. "What's that supposed to mean?" I ask. "Foreclosure, still?"

She shakes her head. "Not imminently, no. Today was a very, very good season opener. The grant money paired with the harvest revenue should more than cover your back payments and start to chip away at the interest a bit. But, you all knew the principle was extremely high…"

Ethan nods. "We knew. But I thought this would be enough going forward. The strawberries and having all the vendors here this spring…"

I can almost see my brother thinking, "What would Grandad do?" But then he seems to toss the thought away, focusing on Lia instead.

He pulls her close and presses his lips to her forehead. My brother relaxes against the love of his life.

Lia continues. "We need to regroup. Maybe restructure the business. There isn't enough space here to do what we need."

Ethan nods. Gran sighs. Samuel kicks a table. What would I do if I were in Ethan's shoes? Well, that's an exercise in futility, because I'm not in his shoes, nor will I ever be.

Grandad saw to that.

"Let's all plan to meet again and discuss some options. We've got another week of peak strawberry madness, and then we can debrief."

Gran and Colleen get to their feet, so I take my cue to go. But when I turn, I nearly knock into Molly.

"Hey." She gives me a bright smile. "Since you're here, wanna see Vaniel?"

"Vaniel?" Okay, I can guess who Vaniel is—who names their vehicle?—but I don't want to seem too excited to see her van. That would be too weird, right?

"My van. Come on, I'll show you."

CHAPTER 6
MOLLY

ALEX HAS TO DUCK HIS HEAD TO GET INTO MY VAN, EVEN WITH his boots off. Being made in miniature sure has its advantages —I'm certain Alex wouldn't fit in my bed.

Not that I'm going to test that theory out, mind you.

I point behind him. "The front seats are storage areas when I'm parked. Then over here," I continue, waving my arms, "is my kitchen-slash-bathroom-slash-pantry-slash-clos-et." Alex does a full turn to face Vaniel's back end. His eyes roam over everything: the white cabinets that I love, the gray subway tiles, the propane stove. That last one I'm really thankful for right now. If I'd gone electric, I wouldn't be able to cook with my batteries on the decline. It is a pain to deal with propane, though. I have to ventilate it properly and the tank I store is really small, so I have to refill frequently.

Alex looks at me, one eyebrow raised. "Bathroom?"

I grin and grasp the handle of the deep bottom drawer on Vaniel's right side. I pull it out and showcase the composting toilet with a wave of jazz hands.

"It's clean, I promise. Ethel's letting me use the bathroom in the pole barn."

Alex crouches down. "How does this work?"

Huh. Most non-vanlifers I meet have zero interest in

learning about my bathroom, if they're not flat-out grossed out by it.

I lift the lid to show him how liquid and solid waste separates and then show him the clean bucket with the actuator, which turns the compost. I pull out my composting bags for the solid decomposed waste and explain that the liquid waste goes into a toilet at the next convenient location—or into the soil if I'm out in nature.

"What do you use for your carbon?"

I show him the coco fiber. "Do you compost on the farm?"

"Of course," Alex says, turning the package over and reading the back. "But first, we have a digester in the back which vents off biogas, and then we turn the digested waste into compost."

"What do *you* use for your carbon?" I can't believe I'm having a conversation with my new boss about composting and poop.

"Mostly bedding, hay, or spoiled feed. In the summer, we can supplement with fresh corn stalks from local farms. We have a program for our neighbors who don't treat their lawns to bring their raked leaves to us in the fall. If we have to supplement, we use biochar."

"What's a digester?" I ask, circling back.

Alex looks up at me. "I'll show you next week, if you want."

"Sure," I say, hands on my hips. When Alex stands, I nudge the drawer closed with one foot and turn. "This is my office-slash-dining-room-slash-bedroom." On each side of the van are two seats against the wall. The one on the right side has a pivoting table to turn it into my office. Past that, up against Vaniel's back doors, is my bed. It's really more like a daybed, a single (custom) mattress with walls enclosing three sides. "I have a board I can place here"—I indicate the space between the two seats—"and then a pillow and foam topper that I can spread out to make a bigger bed for two. But I rarely do that since it's just me. And then I don't have to worry about putting it away every time I want to sit down at my table."

"An office? For work?"

"Well, yeah. But it's mostly for when I video chat with my dad or with friends. Like, I have a book club that meets once a month, so I sit here to talk to them."

Alex puts his large palm on the tabletop and bends down to look at the bottom side. He moves the table around experimentally. It's a special table that can fold down but also can swing around three-hundred-and-sixty degrees. When Alex discovers this, he crouches to look at the mechanism.

I fold my arms on my chest and watch him, one corner of my mouth curled up in a smile. He's curious, and I like that about him. During my time on the road, I've found that curious people are the most interesting.

When he finishes inspecting the table, he stands and puts a hand on my bed and presses, like he's testing the mattress. I half expect him to lie down—

"Oh my god," I say, laughing at the image in my head.

"What?"

"Lie down."

"*What?*"

"Lie down on the bed. I wanna see if you fit."

Alex grumbles, but he obliges me anyway, and I think I catch the edges of a smile as he turns to put his head on my pillow. He lays down, tucking his feet flat on the mattress, knees pointed to the ceiling.

"Well, I think it's safe to say you aren't cut out for van life."

"No shit," he deadpans. He moves, but I put out a hand.

"Wait, wait. Let me take a picture, for Ethel."

"Gran doesn't want a picture of me in this bed." His voice is slightly bitter, but he doesn't move.

I have noticed the tension around the Bedd family. Alex

doesn't engage very much with Ethel, and before today I would have called Alex stiff, but he looks even more tightly wound and uncomfortable when talking to his brother.

I snap the picture and pocket my phone again. I'll show it to Ethel in the morning.

"Who's the man?" Alex asks, breaking me out of my thoughts about the Bedd family. He's looking at the ceiling, where I have some photos taped up. Most of them are various places I've been; with my best friends from home canoeing Horseshoe Lake one summer, Cadillac Ranch outside of Amarillo, Four Corners, Mystic Pizza, the furthest east I went, Kittery in Maine.

Alex is talking about the one picture I have with a man in it—my dad. The picture is old, taken a few years ago at a hockey rink where we watched a curling match together. It was before my dad's last major PTSD episode, before we had to adjust his meds. He's doing a lot better now, in some respects. I almost didn't leave on this trip, but Dad kept pushing me to go. Back then, he was still doing stuff with the Wounded Warrior Project. Now, though, he hasn't talked about it in a while, and I'm worried that he's not getting out of the trailer much.

I don't know how much of this is real or how much of it is in my head. I'm worried about my dad, but is it because I'm not there to take care of him?

Which is why I need to complete this trip. If I drive straight home from here, it's about forty hours, but I won't hit all the states, and I definitely won't fulfill my dad's checklist for each one—eat a meal, visit a tourist attraction, and use the restroom.

I counted Four Corners as a tourist attraction for both Colorado and Utah, ate a snack on both sides, and chugged enough water to make me have to pee—twice.

While I may have only spent a few hours in some states, I spent weeks in other states–I boondocked in the deserts of

New Mexico, spent nearly fourteen days in a small beach town in Florida, and hiked part of the Appalachian Trail in Virginia. I've been on the road for six months, and I've lived a whole other life.

It has its costs, though. Once I get back in Spokane, I can see for myself if my dad's taking his meds, meeting up with friends, seeing his therapist, and make sure his prosthetic is still fitting well, and...and, and, and.

"That's my dad," I tell Alex. In the picture, my dad's prosthetic is visible, so I explain. "He lost his leg in the Gulf War." I perch on the edge of the bed, putting my palm behind me and leaning back so I can look up at the photo. We're not touching, but Alex stills next to me anyway. "He's actually the reason I'm living in the van."

"How so?"

"First of all, the trailer he lives in now isn't much bigger than this. Getting used to living in small spaces wasn't a problem. But mostly it's because when I was a kid, he checked out a book from the library for me called *The Mystery of the Black Raven*. It was part of a series called Boxcar Children. Have you heard of it?"

"Vaguely."

"So, these kids had a boxcar in their backyard that was their playhouse. And I *loved* that idea. My world was small growing up in a trailer park, and for them to have their own space was just wild to me. But we ran out of books at the library and Dad couldn't always get reliable work. So, he started making up stories for me. The series was called 'Molly-girl and Satoot.' Satoot was my Husky stuffed animal, and in the stories, Molly-girl and Satoot lived in a shipping container that would travel all over the world."

I look down at Alex, and he's watching me intently. "I looked for a camper van with a pop-up for a long time, one that could sleep two people, but Dad decided he couldn't go."

"Because of his leg?"

"Maybe." I shrug. That was his excuse, but I think it was really more about his mental health, a topic I don't think is fair to unpack onto Alex, my boss and a near stranger. I stand up and brush myself off. "Anyway, you've seen the whole thing now."

Alex unfolds from my bed, and I turn and walk away before he can loom over me.

"Will I see you tomorrow for more strawberries?" I ask as I step into my slip-on shoes and step out of the van. I retrieve Alex's boots, and he sits in the open door and pulls them on.

"Nah, got farm work to do. I'll see you on Thursday." When he's finished tying his laces, he stands. "Thank you for showing me your van. It's very cool."

I brighten. "Vaniel appreciates it. See you Thursday."

Alex walks away and gives a sharp whistle. His truck is in the driveway, and in the dark of night, I see Trixie emerge from Baabara's home and race toward him. He climbs into the truck, and I duck back inside just before the headlights illumi-nate my home so my boss doesn't catch me watching him.

CHAPTER 7
MOLLY

SUNDAY STARTS OFF SLOW BUT PICKS UP IN THE AFTERNOON. WE sell even more strawberries than we did yesterday...so many strawberries, in fact, it gets to be thin in the bushes and a few customers even remark they wish they could buy more. Lia says it's likely that most of these people are city folks headed back after the weekend and hoping to take a bit of upstate home with them.

Just before bed, I remember I need to email the electrician that I've been talking to about replacing the batteries in Vaniel to let him know I'm in town and need him to come by and take a look. I'm hoping he can do that this week before I start working for Alex on Thursday.

Monday morning Ethel takes me into Climax, the nearest town with a grocery store, and I stock up on food. I buy a ton of canned and dry goods so I don't have to make regular trips to the store and can fill the mini fridge with essentials. We also stop in a souvenir shop that sells knick-knacks with the word *Climax!* printed on them...exclamation point included. I buy a snow globe with a phallic-looking cannon, and I occasionally shake it and giggle.

Ethan runs an extension cord out to Vaniel so that I can

run my power-hogging devices like my laptop and my electric kettle. Boiling on the stove is *so much slower*.

However, the electrician has not responded despite a series of desperate emails I have sent over the next few days.

On Thursday morning, I don't have to be at Udderly Creamy 'til nine. I walk to the pole barn and shed my gloves, stopping to inspect my hands. They've always been kinda dry, but I've been having an eczema flare-up lately; the left hand, extending from the lower knuckle of my pinkie down to the lifeline, has gotten red and cracked. I medicate it with a greasy ointment before bed and wear gloves for a few nights until it goes away. It's looking a lot better now, the skin around it pale with the hypo-pigmentation that tells me it's healing.

I wash my hands with my special soap, use the bathroom, and wash my hands again. When I come out, Ethel is striding toward me.

"Good morning," she calls, slowing. "Can I interest you in taking some coffee or tea with me?"

"Sure! Let me get dressed for work, and I'll be over in about fifteen minutes."

"Take your time. I'll have some toast and jam out as well."

My stomach grumbles at the thought of more of Ethel's homemade jam, and I get ready quickly, walking my bike out to park it next to Baabara's palace so that I can leave right after tea.

Ethel's on the front porch, and I pull out my phone as I take a seat in the padded wicker chair next to her. "I have something to show you." I navigate to the picture of Alex in my bed the other night and when I show it to Ethel, she laughs.

"Ah, that boy was always a big one." She chuckles, pouring tea for me, and tops off her own. She gestures to the spread—toast, butter, jam, and some fruit. "When he came to live with us after our son and his wife passed, he was twelve and still pretty scrawny. Ate half the fridge, it felt like, and then next thing we know, he's sprouted like Jack's beanstalk." She settles back in her chair. "Just like with Ethan, the growth spurt was followed by getting a lot more involved in farm life." Her eyes twinkle. "If you ask nicely, maybe I'll show you pictures sometime."

I swallow my buttered and jammed bread. "Yes please." I want to gobble up everything I can about my quiet boss, and every tidbit I get just makes me more and more interested. What was Alex like as a gangly pre-teen? I can't even imagine.

"His grandad gave him a talking to as soon as we realized he was gonna be a big kid. 'Be careful,' my Eugene would say, 'you're bigger than everyone else. Mind your temper or people will fear you.'"

"He seems pretty successful now. The farm is pretty big, right?"

"Oh yes, let's see. He's got just over four hundred milkers —the cows, I mean." Ethel gives me an excessive rundown of all that Udderly Creamy does. I've pieced together quite a bit myself, but Ethel has the inside scoop on everything. I make lots of 'yeah' and 'oh wow'-sounding noises while I eat.

After Ethel's done with the accounting of Alex's farm and I've eaten my fill, she picks up the breakfast dishes and refuses my offer to help clean up. I hop onto my bike and wave goodbye as I peddle down the road for my first day at the dairy farm.

Instead of slaking my curiosity for Alex Bedd, I fear talking to Ethel has only made it worse.

CHAPTER 8
ALEX

"You don't want me to train Molly?" Kit asks, grinning at me. It's Molly's first day on the job, and we're in my office while I gather Molly's paperwork. Between the four of us, we've already milked the cows, shoveled the shit, and had breakfast. Kit's gotten better about waking up on time and also wearing pants, so the mornings have been a lot more enjoyable. "I'm very good at my job," he continues, practically preening.

"You've been doing 'your job' for exactly two weeks. And Friday, you screwed up an order and double-charged someone, and I had to come down and fix it for you."

"I'm better with people."

So true. "I don't think Molly needs training to talk to people. She needs to learn the software and how to stock, which is my forte. Plus, you'll be gone someday and I'm the one who is actually her boss," I point out. "Despite your efforts otherwise vis-à-vis the HR department."

That argument conveniently overlooks the fact that Kit has no plans to leave anytime soon, and when he first came to stay with me, it was for "a month or so." I don't mind at all; I love having Kit around, and it's nice to have extra hands around the farm, especially when I can call someone up and have help in less than five minutes, versus calling Jesús and interrupting his family time or Perry and making him drive the thirty-eight minutes it takes for him to commute.

"Fine," he allows.

I'm a little relieved. Kit can charm the pants of most people, and I don't want him working that charm on Molly.

Because she's my employee, and that would make things weird.

Minutes later, I walk down the driveway to the farm shop. Since I'll be there for a while, I leave Trixie up at the calf hutches with Kit and Perry while they work on minor maintenance tasks. I arrive at 8:55 A.M. to find Molly already here, her bike leaning against the back of the shop while she waits by the door, fiddling on her phone. She smiles when she sees me and salutes. "Hey, boss."

She's wearing jean shorts and a flowy top with no sleeves, and I suspect she'll be cold today since, unlike the barn, the shop stays pretty cool with the air conditioner running.

Now that I've seen her van, which made me feel like a giant, I can't help but think of her as pocket-sized. The shorts sure do make her legs look long, though. Long and strong, with tanned and freckled thighs.

I snap my gaze away from her bare skin and unlock the door. I hope Molly is a quick learner, so I don't have to stay here in this little room with her all day.

Molly bounces in behind me. "No Trixie today?"

"No." I step behind the counter and wiggle the mouse. An abandoned solitaire game comes up, and I swallow back a sigh. Kit plays games because he's bored as fuck back here. However, I don't want to set a precedent with Molly. "No games when customers are in the shop. I know it gets slow sometimes, but if you see someone coming in, don't look bored."

"Got it. Can I read a book if I'm alone?"

"Sure." I show Molly how to log in and how to make sure

the POS is working. I'm running over the merchandise when our first customer pulls into the small parking lot out front. Molly follows me back to the counter. I can feel her standing behind me as we watch two people get out of the car and look around before entering.

The first woman, a curvy brunette, smiles at me, and then her eyes flit about the space. The second woman, shorter and with a side cut who had her hand on the first's back when they entered, meets my eyes, and I give her a chin dip as a greeting.

I once went to a Hibachi restaurant in Albany where the staff shouted "irasshaimase!" any time someone walked in. It was the most uncomfortable dining experience of my life. There is no need to force friendliness, in my opinion.

Behind me, Molly leans on the counter. I return to our lesson in the merchandise, but quietly.

The women grab a dozen eggs and pay. I'm showing Molly how to ring them up when she smiles at them. "It's my first day," she explains. "He's training me."

"Fun job," the shorter woman says, and I tense at the sarcasm.

Molly doesn't notice it. "I know, right?" I've known her less than a week, and I can tell without looking that she's smiling. "It's really beautiful out here, and Alex promised me I could pet a cow later. Plus, I get to take home fresh milk and eggs, and let me tell you, those eggs will blow your mind. Have you ever had farm-fresh eggs?"

When has Molly had our eggs? I told her one perk of the job was getting as many eggs and milk as she wants—she's one tiny person. How much could she consume? I gladly send four dozen eggs a week home to Jesús's family of five— but I was going to send Molly home with some today.

"We belong to a CSA in the city," the woman says stiffly.

"Oh my god, that's so cool. So, you know *exactly* what I'm talking about. What other stuff do you get with your CSA?"

Ten minutes later, I've run another transaction for some milk and a T-shirt. Molly and the formerly surly woman have swapped recipes for garlic scapes, and Molly's given her a flier about our CSA, even though it doesn't service that far south.

"Bye," she calls as they leave. "Enjoy the milk and eggs!"

The next customer is easier—a local I know who works as a nurse at the hospital in Climax and passes us on her way home. We chat for a bit—she eyes Molly but is more interested in the local gossip and takes all my grunts as interest. I think she's also disappointed Kit isn't here, because she looks around and asks after him.

She finally leaves as another couple comes in, this time a man and a woman who is, I'm pretty sure, but I know better than to open my trap, pregnant.

Like, she's about-to-pop pregnant. Years ago, my kid brother Samuel, always super inquisitive, asked a lady in the grocery store if she was having a baby. Mom, harried from having to make an emergency trip to the store with five kids, gave him the dressing down of his life.

I remember her squatting down and gripping his little arms. "Unless you see a baby coming out or the woman says she's pregnant or her water breaks—" Mom had stopped. Looking back, I wonder if she'd been thinking about how water breaking might look an awful lot like peeing your pants, and having to explain the differences to a five-year-old was probably too much to tackle on that day. "No, unless you see a baby or she says she's pregnant, never assume."

That was five years before my parents were in a freak accident. I was twelve when they died, and to this day, memories like this still catch me off guard with a deep ache of grief.

I turn slightly and nearly bump into Molly. This space behind the counter is too small for two. "Why don't you take over?" I mumble.

She lights up. Man, making her smile is so easy.

"Welcome to Udderly Creamy," she calls to the couple. "Can I help you with anything in particular?"

The woman puts her hands on her lower back and blushes. "Sorry, do you have a bathroom?"

Molly looks at me, and I lead the woman into the back. When I rejoin Molly up front, she's come around the counter and is talking to the man.

"We saw a sign for a place called Climax and just had to stop. But we got turned around, and then we saw a sign for fresh eggs, and here we are."

Molly turns toward me. "They're on their baby moon!"

I raise an eyebrow.

"The last vacation before the baby is due," she explains.

I'm pretty sure these people are here for the bathroom and not to make a purchase, so I leave Molly to chat with him. The woman comes out of the bathroom and joins in, and a few minutes later, I catch the phrase, "You might as well stock up while you're here."

Molly gives them a spiel about our farm— verbatim from the flier—and holds up a bottle of milk and some eggs.

"The eggs aren't pasteurized," I call out. "The FDA recommends pregnant women only consume thoroughly cooked eggs, especially if they are unpasteurized. But the milk is pasteurized."

Molly grins at me. "Good to know." She turns to the couple and explains, "It's my first day on the job." This time, it's said with more pride and less embarrassment and received with even more warmth. She starts to ring them up and then freezes. "Oh my god, we have kid's shirts, right?" She darts around the counter, nearly shoving me out of the way. She quickly sorts through the rack of kid's size T-shirts and pulls out the smallest one she can find. It reads, "Grab life by the teats," with a stylized cow on it.

"Oh, how adorable," the woman gushes, and Molly

finishes checking them out and even walks them to the door, waving goodbye as they drive away.

She skips back to the counter, her grin mischievous. "I'm good, right?" She sticks two thumbs out, all bluster and cockiness. "I'm *so* good. I'm gonna smash this job," she sings, adding a dance to it, putting one hand behind her head and shuffling her feet.

Kit gets like this too, and when someone compliments him, he coasts for days on that high. I gruffly tell Molly, "good job," and she beams at me. "Call me if you need anything," I add.

Molly stops dancing. "Wait, what?"

"You're ready. Give me a call if you have any questions."

I've surprised her, and maybe there's a flash of disappointment on her face. She's probably still nervous, but I'm confident she can hold the fort down here better than I can. And on the farm, there's always more work to be done, so as amusing as it is to watch Molly, I've got to get back to my real work before I discover just how much I could like her.

CHAPTER 9
MOLLY

I'm disappointed when Alex leaves, which is weird because he's my boss and I shouldn't want him watching over my shoulder all the time. But the way he interacted with customers was kind of adorable—not conducive for sales, of course, but adorable. A little shy, but his passion for his farm shines through that bashfulness.

I'm not too worried about the job. It seems straightforward enough, and there's only a few dozen products, and most of them are clothes. Alex told me someone restocks the dairy products every day before the shop opens and, based on the customers I've already had this morning, that's where most of the business is.

The farm stand closes from 1 to 2 p.m. for lunch, and I wasn't sure what the situation was, so I packed my own and pull it out at 1:02 after flipping the sign to closed. I could bike back to Vaniel, but that's a lot of work. Otherwise, there are no restaurants near enough to bike, so a sandwich it is.

I also brought a book. Our book club meeting is in a few weeks, but I'm going pretty slowly through this one—a very popular romantasy that my friend from home, Natasha, picked. I'm enjoying the book—who doesn't love a cold elf king with a heart of gold—but a new Stardew Valley update came out and I started a new save, so I'm addicted to that right now. Good thing Ethan ran a power cord for me to run out to the van.

I finish my sandwich and am reading the book when there's a knock on the door and I look up. Kit stands on the other side of the glass, sporting a goofy grin. One hand is across his forehead, shielding his eyes so he can see, and the other holds two aluminum foil packets.

"It's unlocked," I call.

He frowns and leans back, testing the doorknob and grinning again when it opens. "You know the closed sign probably won't deter people who drive up."

"Oh no, I'll have to sell them something if they're that persistent," I deadpan.

Kit raises the aluminum foil packets. "Alex forgot to tell you about lunch. He was late taking his break too, so we'd already eaten by the time we realized you needed to be fed."

I rub my hands together. "Whatcha got?"

Kit sets the food on the counter. It's still warm and the smell of corn and meat wafts up to my nose. "Anna makes us breakfast every morning and then leaves a warm lunch in the oven. I wasn't sure what you'd like, so I brought a veggie taco and an al pastor." Kit points at each.

"Yum. I did already eat a sandwich, but this smells way better." I tug at the foil of the al pastor, and I'm hit with a meaty and spiced scent that makes my mouth water. Much better than my turkey sandwich.

Kit leans against the counter with a smile and watches as I carefully pick up the juicy bundle and take my first bite. "Yeah, Anna is from Oaxaca, and her food is the best. Mexican food—at least the good stuff—is pretty rare around here."

Kit's happy to talk away while I eat. "You're welcome to come up to the big house every day for lunch, but I will warn you they talk shop the whole time. Today's topic was ordering gendered sperm for the cows that are 'ready to work.'" Kit makes air quotes. "I mean, bull sperm isn't exactly palatable table conversation."

I pause, staring at him, mouth full of taco. He chuckles. "Damn, they got me doing it now."

We grin at each other, and then Kit tells me about his day mucking the stalls, turning the compost, and basically doing anything with a shovel or rake. Then he notices the book I'm reading and tells me about the sci-fi book he's stuck halfway through because he works so hard every day and gets up so early he has to go to bed when he normally would read.

I demolish one taco and then, oh, why the hell not, eat the other. Maybe I'm too full for someone who's not gonna nap, but damn, those tacos were good.

"I'll bring you lunch tomorrow, and we can eat in here, away from the sperm chatter," Kit tells me before leaving at two.

The second strawberry weekend at Bedd Fellows Farm goes even better than the first. I see Alex twice a day when he comes to restock the milk, but it's just a brief hello.

The following week flies by, and as I work at the shop, I meet all kinds of interesting people. I ask everyone where they're from and where they are going, and it's fascinating. There's a guy that comes in on Wednesday and buys milk and eggs to feed his family of six up in Saranac. He commutes to the city two days a week, working from home for the rest. I meet a lot of Fork Lick locals. Friday is the busiest day, with weekend warriors passing through on their way up to the Adirondacks and commuters making their way home.

Kit has lunch with me every day, bringing more of Anna's delicious cooking. Occasionally, we get people driving up and coming to the door, and Kit and I wordlessly slip our food under the counter and let them in. By Thursday, I stop putting the closed sign up during lunch, in favor of selling more for Udderly Creamy.

I'm getting worried about Vaniel, though. The electrician hasn't returned any of my calls. If I can't get him to come out and inspect Vaniel, all of my plans are shot to hell. I'll have to start all over again with a new electrician—if I can even find one here.

CHAPTER 10
MOLLY

Friday evening, I close the farm shop down at six and pedal home. The Catskills are gorgeous and comfortable, even in early summer. Biking back to Bedd Fellows is slightly uphill, though, so I am sweating by the time I roll into the driveway.

Just like she's done every day this week, Baabara bleats at me from her pen. Ethel is out on her porch and waves to me. "Molly, come have some wine."

Well, I won't refuse that offer. I park my bike and climb the stairs to the front porch. A book sits on the table next to her, a tasseled bookmark swinging, and a wineglass rests on the arm of her Adirondack chair, beads of condensation glistening on its surface.

"Go on and pour yourself a glass." She nods toward the front door.

Inside, I find Colleen at the big kitchen table, laptop and paperwork in front of her. I greet her and open the fridge, finding a bottle of Chardonnay on the door. I pour myself a glass and then offer one to Colleen.

"Yes please," she groans, rubbing her eyes. "I'm trying to get all my work done so I'll be free this weekend to help with the strawberry pickers."

"You're a teacher, right?"

"Yup, kindergarten."

I pour the second glass and carefully set it near her laptop. "Tell Gran I'll be out in a bit," she says absentmindedly, her focus already back on her work.

I relay the message to Ethel, who tuts. "Poor girl works too hard. And on her salary. The pay they're giving teachers these days is shameful."

"Definitely," I agree. I sip my wine and sigh. It's cold and crisp, absolute perfection.

"By the way, you're invited for dinner on Sunday night. Everyone's invited. I thought it might be nice to celebrate the end of the weekend harvest with an enormous meal."

"Sounds great." I've always been jealous of big families. For as long as I can remember, it's been my dad and me, so dinners are super quiet and usually eaten in front of the TV. I wonder if "everyone" includes Alex. "Can I bring anything?"

Ethel waves the question away. "Absolutely not. Now, did you make any progress on your book today?"

We've been chatting every morning about our books, among other things. I tell her I only managed to read a few more chapters between customers. Ethel reads too, but not the same type of books I do. She reads a lot of non-fiction, whereas I get bored if there's not a romance plot. I tell Ethel about my book club.

Eventually, Colleen joins us, gulping down a big swig of wine and slumping into her chair.

"What are we talking about?"

"Books," I say, and Colleen immediately brightens. We compare our favorite books and scandalize Ethel with our talk of aliens, shifters, and dukes.

Once my glass is empty, I bid them both good night and return to Vaniel.

Another weekend of strawberry selling passes. When the berries on the bushes thin out, we are forced to turn people away. Ethan puts a piece of paper over the strawberry sign that says SOLD OUT.

We count up the money and help the vendors pack up. Lia and Ethan discuss the profits with hushed tones and worried looks on their faces. Ethel disappeared in the afternoon to escape the heat and prepare dinner. Colleen and I are out in the field putting netting up over the strawberries to protect them from birds when Ethel calls out to us. "Almost done?"

"Fifteen minutes," Colleen shouts back. "Ethan, Lia, you hear that?"

Ethan's shout comes out of the barn where they are putting tables and chairs away and tidying up the bathroom. "Yup."

Fifteen minutes later, our hands are clean and we've gathered in the big house. Colleen pours what looks like lemonade, adding fresh mint leaves as garnish. Ethan grabs one before Colleen can shout "hey" and he chugs it. He gives her a grin when she glares at him. "Thanks, Collie."

She sticks her tongue out.

Siblings are weird.

My ex, Oscar, came from a big family: two sisters and three brothers. We dated for a little over a year in high school and had been friends before that, but they never warmed up to me. I always felt like an outsider, never quite getting the jokes, and not knowing how serious to take everyone. It didn't help that Oscar's oldest sister *really* didn't like me. Every time I was over at their house, she complained about me being there. It wasn't enough that I'd been in their lives for years, I still didn't belong.

Thinking about it makes me nervous, but it's not nearly as rowdy here as when Oscar's family got together, with their six kids, most of them teens. Here it's just Colleen and Ethan, two adult siblings. I like them both, and I like Lia and Ethel.

This'll be fine.

We sit at the table. It's big enough for eight, but since there's only five of us, we take the chairs at one end, Ethel at the head. There's a big serving bowl in the center filled with leafy greens. Platters on the sides have salad ingredients: hard-boiled eggs, bacon, tomatoes in shades of red and yellow, cucumbers sliced perfectly thin, croutons *that are warm from the oven*. If we ever ate croutons when I was growing up, it was the kind that came in a bag.

"I have stomach troubles," Lia explains to me. "It's a lot easier for us to do serve-yourself family meals."

"Cool," I say, and we dig in. I load my plate up with a pile of salad and veggies and douse it with a poppyseed dressing. I'm *starving*.

We're all quiet for a bit as we eat. The lemonade is sweet and refreshing, perfect for washing down a summer salad. The tomatoes are unlike anything I've ever tasted.

"This is so good," I tell Ethel after I swallow a big bite. "Especially the tomatoes."

"Thank you, I grew them myself."

My eyes round. "You did?"

"I grew or made almost everything. Not the eggs, those are from Udderly. The bacon came from one of the local farms, and the goat cheese is from the Price Chopper."

My eyes travel over the spread again. There's a lot here. "The croutons?"

"Baked from sourdough I made yesterday."

"Butter," I say, thinking for sure that she didn't make it.

"Churned it myself."

"What?" I say, my voice all high-pitched. "How do you do that? Isn't it exhausting?"

"In a stand mixer. Set it and forget it." Ethel looks so pleased with herself, and I love that for her.

"Dynamite in the kitchen, *and* you have a green thumb," I say. "Where do you grow it all?"

"I have a garden off the side of the house. You can't see it when you drive by because it's between Baabara's house and ours."

I lift a sprig of basil to my nose and inhale. It's so good.

"Now I grew that downstairs."

"Downstairs?"

"Gran has a garden in the basement with grow lights and aquaponics," Ethan says. "It's mostly for herbs."

"Would you like to see it after dinner?"

"Heck yeah," I say. I know nothing about gardens or seasonal produce, so I ask lots of questions. But eventually I get around to the one that's been bugging me since we sat down.

"Where's Alex?"

CHAPTER 11
ALEX

Trixie lifts her head, so I know company is incoming. Sure enough, Kit rounds the corner into my office, puts his hands on his hips, and gives me the stink eye.

He was with me when I called Gran back, which was stupid. I should have waited until I was alone because when I made up excuses not to come to family dinner, Kit looked at me quizzically. I'd said that I had to work, and then also that Kit was here, and then tried to ignore the disappointment in Gran's voice.

She's not lonely, I tell myself. Grandad's gone, but she's got Colleen living with her, and Ethan and Lia are in the cabin and even Molly's nearby in her van.

Maybe I should be jealous of Gran. When Kit's not here, it's just me and Trixie and it gets pretty quiet.

Once I'd hung up, Kit had protested. He wanted to go to my family's farm for Sunday night dinner, but while Kit often gets his way with his charm and smiles, I just as often get my way with my staunch responses. And I really didn't want to see my family.

Now, though, Kit tosses my truck keys in the air. "Come on, buddy. You said you were spending time with me, so let's do it."

"I also said I was working," I point out.

"And now you're done. We need to eat, and I'll take a beer."

When I emerge from the barn, it is later than I thought. The sun's down, dusk hangs in the air, and a light drop in temperature marks the end of the day. Kit tosses me the keys over the truck bed, and we climb in. Trixie hops into the back seat, and we drive into the only establishment open this late in Fork Lick: Tiddy's.

It's a dive, and not a place made for dinner. It serves the kind of food that keeps you from getting too drunk. I move Trixie's bed from the back seat to the truck bed, and she leaps over the tailgate to get in. She'll be snoring before we hit the front door.

At the bar, we order from Franklin Tiddy, the owner. Kit and I order tots and nachos, but Kit adds on an order of the wing burger—a charbroiled-from-frozen patty smothered in wing sauce.

We also order beers. There's baseball on the lone TV, and a few of the locals, who nodded at me when we walked in, are engrossed in the game.

The tots come out hot and greasy, and Kit pops one in his mouth before it can cool enough and plays an internal version of hot potato, sucking wind and fanning his mouth. I hold a tot up and blow on it until I'm out of breath. Then, inhale and blow again. And again.

By the time Kit can swallow and talk, I've popped my tot in my mouth and it's perfectly cool enough to eat. "Every time," I say.

He takes a big gulp of his beer to cool off. "So, we gonna talk about your family?"

"Nope."

"Come on. I know it's been hard since your grandpa died. I bet you're worried about Ethel. Don't you want to see her?"

When I shrug, Kit kicks me under the table. "Fine. I barely

saw Grandad the last few years, even though we were practically neighbors. And now, being around my family…it just brings up bad memories."

Kit nods. "Like your grandpa telling you to get lost."

I focus on swirling a tot through the ketchup. "Yeah."

"Look, I know what your grandpa did was shit. The man didn't have a lot of tact, especially when it came to raising a bunch of kids. The method wasn't good, but the message was. You're a successful farm manager, you run everything by yourself, and that never would have happened if he hadn't, uh, *suggested*, you go elsewhere."

I snort. Suggested is putting it nicely. Grandad reached the end of his rope when I was fifteen and Ethan and I were fighting about farm work again. Teenage boys have a way of getting physical when they need to figure things out, but this fight wasn't that kind. It got nasty. Ethan and I lost our tempers, and Grandad snapped. There was a lot of yelling about how it was his farm, and his word was the law and who did I think I was to argue with him and Ethan? That was the day it became me against the two of them.

The next day, Grandad came to talk to me alone and told me I needed to think about what I was going to do when I left the farm. I hadn't even considered it. This was my family's farm. Where else did I belong?

To pull a line from the English aristocracy, Ethan was the heir, and I was the spare. There were too many chefs in the kitchen.

Kit's pretty good at looking at the bright side, though. "Yeah. True."

This time, when his foot hits my leg, it's an affectionate nudge, not the physical equivalent of calling me an idiot.

"Did you call your brother back?"

I roll my eyes. God, Kit is nosy.

"No."

I move my leg before Kit can kick me again, and then I

deftly change the subject. "What about you? Sick of farm life yet?"

He grins like a pig in shit. "Hell no."

"Not that I'm kicking you out—"

"Of course not. You love me."

"—but any ideas about what you want to do?"

Kit's wing burger arrives, and he takes a huge bite before answering. "I've been talking to my friends back home in Here."

I nod. Kit has some high school buddies that still live back in the small town of Here, which is about an hour west of here. Any time I go to Here with Kit, we spend time with them.

"I have a job offer from Booker to help him with the construction work he does. I enjoy keeping my hands busy. When you kick me out, I might go do that."

"I'm not gonna kick you out," I grunt.

He ignores me. "But I enjoyed talking to customers in the farm shop. So, I wish there was something I could do with people too."

We spit-ball ideas for a while, and when the food's gone, we pay our tab and leave. We've each only had a beer, so it's safe to drive. Kit moves Trixie's dog bed back inside, calling her "spoiled princess" just loud enough for me to hear.

We drive past my family's farm on the way back. It's hard not to notice the house all lit up, and I can just imagine the Rockwell scene inside; Gran's home-cooked meal, my brother with his first love presiding over the table, Colleen and Lia getting along like a house on fire.

Molly's probably in there too, charming my family like she charms my customers.

It makes it all the more depressing when we turn up the driveway to my empty and dark farmhouse.

CHAPTER 12
MOLLY

On Monday, I have breakfast with Ethel again. She's a hoot and alone in the mornings, and she told me she's happy to feed me breakfast. If I didn't have to go to the farm shop, I'd love to hang out with her all day. It makes me feel terrible for asking where Alex was last night.

Ethel got sad, Ethan and Lia exchanged glances, and Colleen stared at her plate. I was worried that I'd made some huge faux pas and ruined the evening. "We invited him," Ethan said gruffly. "He's got work and Kit visiting."

Thankfully, the dinner table conversation recovered, and after dinner, Ethel showed me her sourdough starter and her basement garden.

In fact, that's what I am missing out on today by going to work: Ethel's agenda is gardening and baking bread.

"I make two, and I'll save you one," she says while I sip my tea.

"Two slices," I say.

"Half a loaf," she negotiates.

"Between you and Alex, I'm well-fed every day. What am I going to do with a half a loaf? Just give me two slices for my evening sandwich."

"Fine, two slices," Ethel allows, and then changes the subject. "Have you heard from your electrician?"

Ugh. "No," I say sullenly. He was so responsive via email, and we had an entire strategy laid out for changing the batteries, and now he's ghosting me.

"You should talk to Alex about it," Ethel suggests. "He's got all those solar panels, and someone must have done that work."

I brighten up. "That's a good idea." I had noticed the solar panels on the roof of the barn and surely there are batteries somewhere. I haven't explored the farm enough to find them. Plus, Alex had said he was going to show me his digester, too.

I really need to get started on the battery upgrade. Ordering components and making a plan takes time, and I'm giving up hope of this electrician ever getting back to me. The clock is ticking.

"While you're at it, maybe you could ask him to Sunday night dinner."

Ethel holds my gaze, tilting her head slightly to gauge my reaction. Oof. I really don't know the protocol here. It feels like sticking my nose in the family drama, and I do *not* know how to do that. And I'm working for both farms, so that's putting me between a rock and a hard place.

"I'll think about it."

I bike to the farm. The weather is getting warmer, and I break a sweat this time. I am not sure what I'm going to do as summer progresses. The bathroom in the farm shop is only a half bath. I have baby wipes somewhere for emergencies since I don't always have access to a shower while on the road, so maybe that's a good start.

There are a few familiar faces throughout the morning, but I'm unfamiliar with most people who stop by. At one, I flip the sign over to closed and intercept Kit coming halfway down the driveway with our lunch on two foil-wrapped plates.

"I have to talk to Alex," I tell him. "Let's eat lunch up there?"

Kit does an about-face. "Sure."

For the first time, I step inside the house. Kit and I immediately toe off our shoes in the mudroom, adding to the pile of dirty work boots. It's a log-cabin style home, and the kitchen is right off the entrance to the right. It's a galley kitchen, and Kit leads me through it, following voices into the dining room. The table is long with benches on either side, and the men around the table have paused their eating to watch us come in. Kit introduces me to Perry, the lean, older white man, and Jesús, a shorter, stockier Latino man.

"Please, no sperm talk," I joke.

Alex chokes on his food. He raises his fist to his mouth, and his cheeks bulge out, trying to contain whatever they're eating—there's an enormous platter of it in the center of the table, and it smells divine.

Perry puts a hand on his shoulder, concern etching his face. "Boss?"

Alex waves away the help, finally swallowing and turning away to cough properly. The side of his neck and his ears are red.

Finally, he gets control of himself and gulps some water. He wipes his face on a cloth napkin from his lap and looks up at us. "Why on *earth* would we talk about sperm?"

Kit raises a long leg and climbs over the bench, settling in at an empty seat next to Alex. "You talk about sperm *all the time.*"

Alex sputters, eyes glancing to me and back to Kit. "Do not."

Jesús moves slightly on the bench and gestures for me to sit next to him, across from Alex.

Over the noise of the aluminum foil coming off our plates, Kit rebuts, "Just this morning, you and Jesús were talking about how many straws you wanted to order next."

"Straws?" I ask.

"Tube of sperm," Kit explains. "You should see these cata-logs, Molly. They tout the teat size for the heifers, the scrotal circumference for bullies—"

"I thought you didn't want to talk about sperm?" Alex interrupts.

"Right. So, what were you talking about?"

Perry snorts.

Alex mumbles something.

Holding a hand up to his ear, Kit says, "What was that now?"

"The next AI round for the Nigerians."

Kit grins and then translates for me. "The next round of artificial insemination for the Nigerian Dwarf goats."

I chuckle and then take a bite of my lunch—an enchilada-looking thing smothered in a thick, dark sauce. I close my eyes and moan. Fuck, Anna's meals are so good.

When I open them, Alex is staring at me. No—staring at *my lips*.

The heat in his gaze sends a shiver down my spine.

Kit, Jesús, and Perry are discussing something, but I'm not paying attention. I'm too busy savoring this delicious meal and stealing glances at Alex.

He's watching me right back, our eyes occasionally meeting and darting away again. Alex is such a big man, hunched over his plate while he eats, one forearm resting on the table with his sleeves rolled up.

I like his gaze on me. I like it a lot.

"Could you help me?" I ask quietly, just to Alex.

He lowers his fork and tilts his head slightly.

"I had this guy lined up to replace my batteries. We'd emailed and agreed on a plan and a budget, but he never sent me any type of contract. He's stopped answering my emails, though."

"What was his name?"

I tell Alex, and his mouth twists. "Consider yourself having dodged a bullet. His work is shit."

My shoulders slump. "Fuuuuucccckkk. Is there anyone else who could do it?" Finding an electrician in a big city is easier, but I'd have to find a safe place to park and live in my van, and right now, my free parking at Bedd Fellows is a really good deal.

Plus, if I don't stay, I'll be putting both farms in a bind.

Alex grimaces. "You're only here, what? Two more months? Short notice'll be hard."

"I know." I frown down at my food and twirl my fork through my sauce.

Alex's gaze moves over me, and his eyebrows drop. "Let me make some calls."

I give him half a smile. "Thanks. Also…" I glance over at the other men, but they're deep in conversation about—baseball, I think? "You don't have to tell me any details, but like… you didn't come to Sunday dinner. Is your family…bad?"

"Bad?"

"You know, like narcissists who you're better off being no contact with? Emotionally abu—"

Those brows drawn down even farther. "No. *No.*" He says the second one so emphatically that Kit glances over. We eat for a few moments and Alex says in a low voice, almost under his breath. "I just don't fit in there."

CHAPTER 13
MOLLY

I DIDN'T WANT TO PRY, SO I LET THE TOPIC DROP, BUT THE WORDS echoed inside me for a while.

Meanwhile, Alex puts me in touch with an electrician who comes out on Thursday to look at Vaniel.

Quinn crawls all through the van with me, poking her head in to look at the batteries and the wiring. It's after work, and the sky is darkening, but we have headlamps.

Finally, Quinn hops out and dusts her hands off. She's fit and tall, wearing jeans and a fitted tee, her blonde hair in a ponytail. "It's a fun project," she says. "I can definitely do it."

"Awesome."

"However, I'm going to have to put in the time on the weekends." She grimaces. "I've got a pretty full slate of projects during the week. Does that work for you?"

"I work weekends here on this farm, so I'll be nearby but working. Nights might be easier."

Quinn shakes her head. "Commuting from Here and back means I can't come after my main job."

"From here and back?" I ask, confused.

She laughs. "Here, New York. You know Kit, right? That's where he's from. I work for his best friend, Booker, during the week. It's an hour each way."

"Oof, that's a long drive. I hope it'll be worth it."

Quinn lifts her bag of tools into the back of her truck. Now, I'm worried about paying for her mileage and drive time, on top of the work.

She laughs again, seeing my face. "Don't worry. My rates are very reasonable, and Alex mentioned that if I come down, he has a few small jobs for me, and you can split the travel costs."

"Okay, that's better."

"Plus, I'll get to see Kit." She grins. She smiles a lot, and I like her.

"Are you two…?"

"Definitely not. Kit's fun, but he's not my type. Fortunately, I figured out he wasn't early on, because that man leaves a trail of broken hearts everywhere he goes. But he's good to have a drink with, and I like Alex too. They might even let me spend a few Saturday nights at the big house, so I don't have to drive back."

I wonder what Alex is like when he's relaxed and with friends. Does he open up? Do he and Kit balance each other out? Or is Kit where everyone's attention goes, and Alex fades into the background?

Quinn heads out. When she emails me with the estimate, it's slightly over what I agreed to with the electrician who ghosted me. But, as much as the Bedd family—on both farms —is feeding me, I think I can make it work.

I sell so much at the farm shop on Friday that in the afternoon, I have to call Alex to let him know we're almost out of eggs and whole milk. He doesn't answer. I mentally kick myself for not getting Kit's number, as often as we've been hanging out.

Another commuter comes in and buys eggs, so I call Alex again. Still no answer. Frustrated, I slap a "back in ten" sign on the door and lock up.

I wish I could whistle, like Kit did to get Alex here the day I came for my job interview. Maybe I should carry a whistle with me to get Trixie's attention.

I trudge up the hill and into the barn. With the cows out in the field, it's empty and quiet. I walk down the main aisle until I hear voices and follow the sound until I exit the barn out the far side. There's a series of what looks like dog crates but much bigger, each one fenced in and containing a baby cow or two.

Holy hell, they are stinking cute. "Oh my god," I coo at the nearest one, who ambles over to the metal barrier, ears flicking and huge brown eyes staring at me.

Dad always told me anything with a mouth can bite, so I don't poke my finger in the cage to scratch it like I want to. The calf lips at the wire, and its little tail flicks, and I almost die of a cuteness overload.

I'm glad no one can see me as I babble at the animal. "Who's a cutie? Oh my god, you are a cutie. Yes, such a widdle baby with your big ears and eyes, and oh my, what big eyelashes you have."

I sound like a fairy tale villain. I make a few more kissy noises and straighten up. There are dozens of calves in these pens, each cuter than the last. Most pens even have two inside, and when I walk past, they compete for my attention, nudging each other and following me from one side to the other.

Dear god, it's like a pet store. And somehow, the baby cows are even cuter than kittens or puppies. How did I not know this?

I wonder if any of them are going to be eaten, but I don't think Udderly sells meat. I also remember Kit mentioning gendered sperm, so I wonder if these are all girl cows. Does Alex name them? I can understand not naming the cow who's going to be on your plate, but these are "milkers" as I keep hearing them referred to, so do they get names?

I'm following the voices, lost in my thoughts, totally unprepared for what I see when I turn the corner.

CHAPTER 14
ALEX

PERRY AND I ARE DEEP IN CONVERSATION DISCUSSING COLOSTRUM and weaning that I don't even notice Molly coming around the corner until she gasps.

Perry and I both jerk, and my heart rate spikes, worried that the gasp is in pain or fear, but when I get a look at Molly's face, I relax. She's fine, but stares at the baby goat in my arms, feeding from the bottle I'm holding.

"Afternoon, Molly," Perry says.

She doesn't answer but slowly, glacially, sinks to her knees. Perry starts forward, concern etched on his posture, but stops short, flummoxed.

Molly's hands come up to her face, holding her cheeks as she gapes at me—well, at the kid. "What is happening? How can anything be that cute? I can't take it! Cuteness overload. I'm melting."

Perry laughs, the wrinkles around his eyes deepening.

To be fair, I am immune to cuteness overload, having been around baby animals my whole life. But I like this response from Molly. Maybe I should hold and bottle-feed premature baby goats every day.

Nah, that's a dumb idea. This is cuteness, not sexiness. Or

does cuteness like this increase sexiness? I don't know; maybe I'll ask Kit.

To my alarm, tears are forming in Molly's eyes. Oh no, she really can't handle the cute.

"It's so small," she says, her voice barely a whisper.

One hand holds the bottle, but I lightly stroke the kid's flank with my other hand. "Would you like to pet her?"

Molly is by my side in a flash. Her hands are still up on her face, though, and I notice she's got a red, dry spot on the pinky side of her palm. "How should I pet it? Why is it so tiny?"

Out of the corner of my eye, I see Perry slip away. It's just me and Molly out here in the kid pens, though I think she hasn't even noticed that she's literally surrounded by baby goats.

Molly's close to me. Really close. I can see the freckles across her nose and the sky blue of her eyes and the prism of colors in her red hair—it's not bright red, but she's got lighter hair, almost blond, at her temples and a deep, auburn shade behind her neck.

I shake myself mentally and focus back on the kid in my arms. "She's pretty happy right now, drinking from the bottle, so you can pet her just like a cat."

Molly does as instructed, stroking the back of the kid with her entire hand. The bottle's almost empty.

I look back up at Molly and her tears have spilled onto her cheeks. "I have literally never seen anything cuter," she tells me, wiping her cheeks with the back of her free hand. She keeps stroking, and occasionally she brushes against my forearm or my flannel-covered chest. I feel every touch through the animal in my arms; the slight weight of Molly's affection, the warmth of her standing beside me, even on this summer's day, and the stroke of her skin, even accidentally, against the hair on my forearm, as if I'm being petted too.

I clear my throat. Right. Molly had asked some questions.

What were they? Oh, right. First one: answered. Second one. "She's so tiny because she was premature." I explain her birth and how we weren't sure she was going to survive. She drinks slower than she should at her age, and she's pretty low energy. But I think she's going to make it. Molly gets brave enough to stroke the kid's little head, running a finger over the tiny poll and soft ears.

The kid releases the nipple, causing a few drops to soak into my flannel, and squirms. That's a good sign, and it breaks the tension between me and Molly.

I place the animal back in its pen, and it ambles away, nosing the ground and then pooping. Molly peers in the cage. "Where's its mom? Why is the poop yellow? I have so many questions."

"It's milk poop," I explain, and when Molly stares at me blankly, I explain that the color changes depending on what the goat eats. Then I tell her we separate the babies after a few days to take better care of them than the mothers and increase the dam's milk production. And for their own safety—the sad reality is that baby goats with their dam or other dams is dangerous.

"That makes sense, I guess. They are working animals." She looks around, noticing the other kids. "Are these ones older?"

We walk down the corrals for a while, me squinting at the numbers on the gates and telling Molly how old each one is. Since we breed en masse, most of the kids are about the same age, give or take a few days. The kid I was feeding is from the second insemination round for the dams that didn't take on the first one.

"Alex," Kit's voice calls from the barn. "You left your phone in the office again." He strides toward us, tossing me my phone when he gets close enough, and he and Molly grin at each other. Trixie circles the three of us, gives a huff in greeting, and then sniffs the pens. "Hey, Perky."

"Perky?" I ask. When did he give Molly a nickname?

Molly rolls her eyes. "That's what some of my friends call me. Short for Perkins, obviously. Mr. Nosy here saw one of them texting me and thinks he's in my inner circle now." She hip-bumps Kit, and he slings an arm around her.

I frown and try to ignore the jealousy in my gut. Kit's friendly to everyone. And so what if they like each other? I'm her boss. I can't get mad about something that is none of my business.

Unlocking my phone, I see that I have missed calls from the farm shop, Gran, and my brother, Ethan. I swipe them all away, plus some notifications for a few of our social media accounts. Instagram is always trying to get me to post more, but I never do. I glance back up at Molly. "You called me?"

Molly's face falls. "Oh shit, I left the shop unattended. I put a sign up that I'd be back," she rushes to add. "I just didn't expect to be gone for so long. We need more eggs and whole milk."

My eyebrow raises. "Already?" I've usually had Kit run down at the end of the day to grab the unsold products. I also check our sales reports for the shop every day, and I've noticed that sales have gone up. They were higher than normal the week Kit was at the counter, but they're up even more since Molly has been there. At least, compared to when I had a sign on the door to call for service, which isn't a surprise. I increased the Friday morning stock in anticipation, so being almost sold out of a few things surprises me.

"Yeah. There have been quite a lot of big purchases today. A few people came in and said they won't be able to make it to the strawberry picking this week, but they wanted to get some fresh milk from you because the one they had last week was so good. And someone came by—Lionel, I think—told me to tell you hello. His daughter is visiting with her kids, and he bought a lot."

Lionel is the only lawyer in Fork Lick, the one who

executed Grandad's will. That makes me think about the missed calls from my family, and I sigh. "Alright, I'll send one of the guys down in a few with a restock."

Molly brightens, befitting her nickname. "Thanks, boss." She pats Kit's chest. "Catch you later, Romeo."

Romeo? God damn it. I'm jealous of my best friend.

CHAPTER 15
MOLLY

IN BETWEEN CUSTOMERS, I SPEND THE AFTERNOON THINKING about Alex holding that damn goat. What is it about a big, burly guy, beard and flannel and work boots, holding a baby goat that makes my heart go pitter-patter?

It must be all those mountain men romance books I've read. They're thick with beards and flannel, but not so much baby goats—a major oversight, in my humble opinion.

I leave work and bike home, waving hello to Ethel out on the porch. After dinner, I call my dad.

"Hey, Molly-girl, how was your week on the farm?"

I fill him in on all the shop news—the delicious food, the people I talked to, the baby animals I met. I've sent Dad pictures every day. Just because I'm not actively on the move doesn't mean I'm not having an adventure that I can share with him. He's probably never petted a baby goat before, so I tell him everything I learned.

This was the deal we made. Dad came home from deployment missing a leg, then received divorce papers and a two-year-old girl to take care of while my mother ran off with another man and never looked back.

The Boxcar Children and the stories my dad made up

were some of my earliest memories, and according to him, all I talked about as a kid was wanting a boxcar of my own.

After the last business I worked for closed, Dad said life was short, and I had to take my savings and go now. All those conversations we had, dreaming about what Molly-girl and Satoot were doing, became real.

"I didn't take any pictures," I say regretfully. "Didn't take my phone with me. Next time, I'll get some photos."

"I bet you'd look real stinking cute petting a goat."

Not as cute as Alex did, I think. Seriously, seeing his big arms, with the sleeves rolled up and the light hair and tanned skin on display, was sexy enough, but goddamn, that baby goat took me down. I'll never look at the man the same. And holding a bottle? Nursing a baby of any species? My ovaries exploded, and I was pretty sure they had been in a deep slumber. I've never thought dad-qualities would be sexy, but here we are. Not that I want kids all of a sudden, but thinking of Alex as a dad is pretty sexy.

Though, look, I'm not a huge baby fan. Alex holding a baby goat, even if it poops yellow, is way more attractive to me than a wailing, fussy baby. This goat was three days old and when I left, it was romping around, bouncing off the walls of its little pen.

My understanding (limited as it is) is that baby humans don't do that until they're about two years old? Three? I don't know. I occasionally hang out with vanlifers my age who have young kids, but I'm out of my depth.

"Molly-girl? You still there?"

Whoops.

"Yeah, Dad, sorry. Anyway, enough about the farm. Are you going to the rec center tonight?" Dad usually goes to the veterans' rec center on Friday nights to meet up with his buddies and play games.

"Nah, not tonight. I've got other stuff to do."

"Oh? Whatcha doing?"

Dad lists a few chores and an episode of something on TV he wants to watch, but he says it all in that hemming-and-hawing way that lets me know he's lying. Well, maybe not lying to me, but lying to himself. He does have all those things to do, but he's using them as an excuse not to get out of the trailer.

"Those things can all wait. You should go play pickleball. You need to get out more."

"Don't worry about me. I'll be fine."

Dad makes an excuse to go, and worry gnaws at me. His meds have been effective lately, but when his mental health declines, Dad doesn't leave the trailer much.

That's the worst part about being on my trip. I have to remind myself that my dad is a grown man with resources, medication, and friends. I just hope all that's enough.

I hang up with Dad and get ready for bed. All the while my thoughts keep drifting back to Alex.

I haven't been with a guy in almost a year. That must be why I find myself reaching for my vibrator once I'm under the cover. This whole van trip has been a bit of a sexual awakening for me—not because I've been bringing home men, but because, for the first time, I'm not living under the same roof with my dad.

I still have to be quiet because Vaniel's walls are *not* soundproof. In other places, I don't need my fellow vanlifers listening in. Here, I don't want Ethan and Lia or whoever else might be wandering around overhearing me when they walk between their cabin and the big house.

It's not until after I turn out the lights and get myself off thinking about mountain men in flannel that I realize I didn't ask Alex to Sunday dinner. Ethel hasn't asked about it, but I get the feeling that she's lonely during the day. She's always so glad to see me when I bike up the driveway.

Saturday morning, when Alex drops off the milk, I walk

him back out to his truck. "Hey, you should come to dinner on Sunday night."

Alex looks at me out of the corner of his eye. "Sunday night dinner again?"

"Yeah. It was so good last week. Ethel's going to make fresh bread tomorrow and says she got a batch of asparagus from one of the neighbors. Did you know it takes two or three years to harvest the first crop of asparagus? And they grow right out of the ground like this?" I demonstrate with my hand and a finger.

Alex doesn't respond to my asparagus rambling, but I can practically hear the gears turning in his head. Just before he gets to his truck, he whistles for Trixie, who comes sprinting out of the sheep palace. "I've still got Kit with me, and I work late sometimes on Sunday."

"Bring Kit," I say, hoping Ethel won't mind.

Alex opens the door to his truck, shaking his head. "Some other time."

"Fine," I grumble. "See ya Monday."

But I see Alex a few hours later. Usually, he sends someone else over to Bedd Fellows to pick up the ice chest for the milk to be refilled. The first time he sent Kit, who lingered for an hour talking to people until Ethan kicked him out for eating too many strawberries. From then on, Alex sent Perry or Jesús, but today he comes himself.

We're alone out here. We all helped the vendors pack up, and then Colleen took the money inside. Ethan and Lia are out in the field cleaning up. I've been stacking buckets at my table.

I sold the last milk bottle in the early afternoon, and I'd just been thinking that Alex should bring more in the morning, and that gives me an idea. I'm not sure this is a good idea —getting involved more with the Bedd family—but I go with it anyway. I'm leaving at the end of the summer, how bad could it get? It wouldn't be like Oscar and I and our teenaged angst.

"Hey, Alex."

He raises a brow at me.

"Do you have another ice chest?"

He lifts it up by one handle now that he's emptied it of ice. "This big?"

"Yeah."

He nods.

"Fill it and bring it tomorrow. I bet I can sell it all."

The second eyebrow joins the first. "Which kind?"

I roll my eyes. "The strawberry, duh." It always sells out first, and I know he didn't want to make it at all.

"What's the bet?"

"If I win, you come to Sunday dinner. If I lose...I'll..." I cast about for something Alex might want from me.

To my shock, Alex's eyes dip to my lips. My stomach flips. Is that what he wants? A kiss? When his eyes meet mine again, he's blushing, and his gaze darts away quickly.

I put my palms on the tabletop and lean in. "If I win, you come to dinner tomorrow. If I lose, I'll kiss you."

Alex goes absolutely stone still. I realize what I've done. I just propositioned my boss. What was I thinking?

I wasn't, obviously. I need the money to pay for the batteries. I need to get my paycheck every week so I can pay Quinn as much as I can. My mouth has run away from me, but for a moment, I forgot Alex signs my paycheck and that he could fire me for inappropriate behavior.

Why do I always do this? From milking virtual cows to baby goat cuteness overload, I just can't seem to keep my mouth shut around Alex.

Just when I'm about to blurt out a backtrack, Alex swallows. "Okay."

Before I can say anything else, he bends down, grabs the ice chest, and stalks off.

Watching him leave, I realize that I've put myself in a really dumb position.

Because now I kind of want to lose.

I don't lose. Strawberry production is high this week and we stay open longer than last week. I offer samples of the strawberry milk and really work it with the parents. *Strawberries grown right here on the farm, never frozen. The dairy cows are raised in a pasture right down the road.* Ethel and I talked about the recipe recently, so I'm educated enough to say things like, *the syrup is made right over there by the farm's owner,* while I point to the big house. Ethel told me to make everything above board, she has a home processor exemption so she can legally sell the syrup and her jams. When the strawberries dwindle, I've got strawberry milk to sell, and I sell the whole damn lot.

For the first time, I text Alex.

MOLLY

Guess who's coming for dinner tonight??

ALEX

Okay.

I grin, hearing Alex's gruff voice in my head. Texting gives me no context clues as to how he feels about losing, but I think I've figured out a happy compromise.

I run off to tell Ethel.

"Really?" she asks, hand to her chest.

"Oh, Kit too, maybe."

Ethel waves it away. "We've got plenty of food."

"Okay, I'm gonna finish clean-up. Smells great in here, by the way."

I rush back to clean the pole barn bathroom and then

check on Vaniel. Quinn's been here, and while she's tidied up, it's a small space and thus contains barely controlled mayhem. The old batteries are still online; she's getting the entire system set up first, and then when she's ready, we'll shut everything down and swap to the new batteries.

It sounds so simple when I think of it like that, but I have a healthy fear of being electrocuted, so I am very glad that I found Quinn.

I'm back in the house carrying a bean salad to the table when the door opens, and I hear an enthusiastic Kit. I hang back while Ethan and Colleen greet their brother. He has to bend down to hug Ethel.

We finally sit down to eat, passing big platters of food around.

Ethel catches my gaze, and her eyes twinkle. "What do you think, dear?"

I tap my chin, surveying the food. "Bread, obviously. Green beans, tomatoes, umm…what's the leafy green?"

"Arugula."

Alex, sitting next to me, leans over. "What are you doing?"

"I'm guessing which parts of the meal Ethel grew or made. I'm sure you didn't make the chicken." There's a platter of grilled chicken being passed around. I notice Alex doesn't take any. "What about the beans?"

"Fava, from out in the garden."

"And what's that?" I point at the pile of sauteed greens in a bowl.

"Chard."

"Also from the garden." I decide.

Alex hands me the bread. "The garden looks much better than it did this winter, Gran."

"Thank you, dear. Anything else, Molly?"

I squint at her. "No?"

She shakes her head with a grin. "Made the butter again."

"Dang it. I always forget about the butter. Making it just

seems so old-school to me. Well, so does the bread, but I think it's more believable for some reason. Maybe all those Covid bakers got me used to the idea. I didn't hear about anyone making butter." I tap my chin. "You can't even make it in Stardew Valley, even though the cheese machines look like butter churners."

Alex coughs. "Cheese machines?"

"Yup. Just goat cheese and cow cheese. Wait, have you made cheese, Ethel?"

"Not in a long time," she says. "It's a lot more complicated than butter."

Man, Ethel is a wealth of knowledge. It's the kind of experience that's probably dying out. I wonder if they still teach that kind of stuff in home economics. Probably not, considering the state of the school system. Maybe they teach it in ag school.

I turn to Alex. "Have you ever made cheese?"

"Of course."

"But you don't sell it."

He shakes his head.

We all fall quiet for a minute, eating our delicious farm-grown meal, until Alex interrupts. "How's school, Collie?"

"I'm not a dog!" She makes a face at her brother but then updates the table on her volunteer work at the library, which leads to Kit telling ridiculous stories of himself as a boy. There's a lull in the conversation at the first mention of Alex's mom, who Ethel told me passed away about eighteen years ago, but then Ethan brings up a story about their brother, Samuel, getting picked on in school and how the older brothers played bodyguard until Samuel put a homemade stink bomb in the bully's lockers.

Ethel serves strawberry crumble, pointing out to Lia that it's gluten-free.

A sudden pang hits me. I wish my dad was here. Instead, he's thousands of miles away, all alone.

CHAPTER 16
ALEX

DINNER GOES BETTER THAN I EXPECT IT TO. WHEN SAM AND Jackson were here in February for the service and the reading of the will, we all got together, but it felt different. It felt morose, with the one-two punch of Grandad having passed away and learning about the farm's debt.

When Jackson and Sam left, we all returned to our defaults as if nothing had changed—they went back to their lives, and I went back to the farm.

Looking at Ethan now, he's not back to his default. My older brother looks happy and more talkative. With seven of us here, he's at the head, opposite Gran, where Grandad used to sit.

Look, he's become the patriarch of the Bedd family, just like Grandad knew he would.

Before I can get too into my head about it, Gran gets up to gather plates, and the rest of us stand up in protest. Colleen quickly picks up Gran's wineglass and refills it, telling her to go sit somewhere and enjoy her book. Ethan starts loading the dishwasher while Lia and Molly pack up leftovers. Once the dishes are all loaded, Ethan switches to hand washing the pots and pans, and I grab a kitchen towel, ready to dry.

The women filter out, not all the way to the porch where

Gran sits, but I can hear them talking in the living room. Kit lingers, sneaking pieces of Gran's sourdough.

"So, does this mean you'll return my calls now?" Ethan asks.

I grunt and glance over at Kit. He pretends not to be listening and crams another chunk of crust in his mouth. "We're talking now, right?"

Ethan smiles into the suds and shakes his head. "Come on, let me take you out to lunch this week. Tomorrow? Tuesday?"

"He can do Tuesday," Kit pipes up.

"What, you know my schedule?"

"Am I wrong?"

I sigh. "Fine. Tuesday."

"Good, I'll pick you up at noon. We'll go into town."

That means we're going to Lick Your Fork, the diner that's been a Fork Lick institution since I was a kid.

"Fine," I say.

Once he's got my assent, Ethan asks Kit about his work options, leaving me to dry Gran's vintage Pyrex dishes and new wine glasses.

I should be thinking about my upcoming conversation with Ethan, but instead, I'm thinking about that stupid bet Molly and I made earlier. Did she offer the kiss because she knew she was gonna win? I was fairly certain she was going to lose, but I guess I'd been selling out faster than I'd thought.

All day, though, I'd been thinking about it. Wondering what she'd say to me after they closed for the day, waiting for that text. It came earlier than I thought, bringing with it crashing disappointment.

I'd never had anyone bet me a kiss.

"Yoo-hoo? Alex?"

My brother's hand waves in my field of view. I jump.

"What?"

Ethan smirks at me. "That was the last one."

Oh. I've just been standing, staring out the dark window, waiting for the next wine glass.

"Gee, what could he be thinking about?" Kit asks wryly.

I shoot him a dirty look over my shoulder while I hang up the towel. I'm about to pinch him when Gran walks in. "Don't mind me, boys, just making a to-go box for Molly so she doesn't have to cook tomorrow night."

She opens the fridge, and behind her back, I deliver that pinch. Kit grimaces and bites his lip, working to stay quiet. Then he grabs a hunk of bread and rips off a bit, flinging it at me and shoving the rest in his mouth.

I catch it with my mouth and grin. When I look back at Ethan, he's smiling at me softly. It hits me like a two-by-four that we used to pinch and throw food at each other right here in this kitchen. And the look on his face makes me think that he's remembering when we used to play more than we used to fight.

"Here." Gran shoves a Tupperware at my chest. "Now go walk Molly home."

Ethan snickers, and Kit strolls into the living room. "Molly, your security officer is here to escort you home."

I walk out with the leftovers, and Molly thanks my Gran for a wonderful night with a hug. She says goodbye to everyone and steps out into the night, waiting for me at the bottom step.

"Wanna see what Quinn's been working on?"

"Sure," I say, and we walk out to Vaniel. Molly hums quietly and looks up at the stars. The sky is clear tonight, the bugs loud, and it strikes me how different the two farms are. Mine is much noisier, even at night, with animals stomping and snorting. Ethan's crops don't make a peep.

In the van, we toe off our shoes, and Molly puts the leftovers in her fridge. The last tour didn't include details on the electrical system, so Molly gives me a bare rundown of how it works. Thanks to government funding, we were able to put solar panels on the south-facing roof of the barn, a project that I largely handled, so I know the basics of how these things work. After Molly walks me through her system, I'm pretty up to speed.

"What're you going to use for your battery management system?"

"Uhhh…" Molly wrinkles her brow in concentration. "I don't remember."

"What about—"

Molly holds up a hand to cut me off. "Maybe talk to Quinn. I understand what she's saying—kinda—while she says it, but it's over my head." She chuckles self-deprecatingly.

I straighten from where I was crouched on the floor and immediately whack my head on the ceiling. "Damn it."

"Oof, you okay?"

I rub it. Nothing but bruised pride. "Yeah." That's my cue to leave.

Molly follows me to the door, which is open but covered with a screen curtain, keeping the bugs out.

I toss my boots onto the nearby grass and sit down at the lip of the floor to tug them on. I get up and turn around, coming face-to-face with Molly, who stands inside the van, holding the screen out of the way.

"Well," I say, rubbing the back of my neck. "I'll see you tomorrow."

Instead of answering, Molly bends over, putting her hand on my chest and freezing me in place. Her lips meet mine in a quick, soft kiss. She tastes like wine and strawberries and warmth. My brain, which has been sputtering a bit every time I've thought about Molly today, full-on seizes.

She straightens up, smiles at me, and lets her hand fall. "Goodnight, Alex. See you tomorrow."

CHAPTER 17
ALEX

ETHAN PICKS ME UP IN HIS TRUCK ON TUESDAY. I CLIMB IN THE cab while Ethan peers out the windshield. Trixie's staying back with Kit today, who waves from the barn.

"Place looks good," Ethan says.

I look back and try to see it with my brother's eyes. It is a good-looking farm—Perry, who's a welder and very handy, keeps the fences in good order, the grass is bright summer green, and the barn's a nice, butter-yellow color. I don't think much has changed since Ethan saw it last, but I'll take the compliment.

"How's Lia?" I ask.

Ethan tells me about taking her to Climax for her infusion last week, talking about her Crohn's diagnosis, and using words like "white blood cell count" and "FOD-MAP diet." I'm lost, but it's clear that my brother has taken the time to educate himself and help Lia.

We pull into the parking lot at Lick Your Fork.

"Well, if it isn't the oldest two Bedd boys," the waitress, Latonya, comments when we walk in. She's been working here as long as I've known her, and one of her grandkids was in Colleen's class a few years back. Her dark skin has deep laugh lines, and her gray hair is up in a tight bun. "Anyone else joining you?"

"Just us, LT," Ethan says.

Latonya leads us to a window booth, plops menus down, and immediately asks what we want.

"Veggie omelet, please," I say.

"Hash browns on the side?"

"Yes, ma'am."

She turns to my brother. "And lemme guess; the special?"

"Please."

Latonya picks up the menus. "You got it, sugar. And tell that lovely young lady of yours that I got new gluten-free buns this week and that we're putting a new salad on the menu. She can have it with the feta cheese on the side."

"Thanks, will do."

I take a minute to scan the diner. It's the only place to eat lunch in Fork Lick, and the food is way better than Tiddy's— no offense to Tiddy. I recognize a few faces and exchange a few head nods.

When I look back at Ethan, he's watching me.

Whatever he's thinking has to wait while Latonya delivers coffee and cream. But as soon as she disappears, Ethan leans forward.

"I could use some advice."

"From me?" The words fly out of my mouth.

"Yeah, from you. You know a lot about farming and the market for fresh products. Your dairy farm is amazing, and so's the milk, by the way. It's definitely a fan favorite over the weekends."

"I can tell," I say wryly, thinking of Molly's bet. I've been trying not to think about Molly too much since that kiss, but twice yesterday, Kit snapped his fingers in front of my face when he didn't think I was paying attention.

He also told me my eyebrows were giving me away again.

I don't know exactly what they were saying, but he just grinned at me.

"So, what advice do you want from me?"

"Well, it was Lia's idea to apply for the grant, but switching from soybean to more diversified crops was something you and Samuel campaigned for ages ago."

"Yeah, well, Grandad didn't listen."

"And look where we are now," Ethan says, his voice growing sharper. "Grandad should have listened to you—*I* should have listened to you instead of thinking he knew best. I don't envy Grandad's life; raising us kids in his sixties and farming is a hard business. But we can't make the same mistakes going forward. We've got...well, we've got our futures to think about."

There's a crease of worry between my brother's eyes, but there's also hope in his words. It smacks me over the head real hard what *our futures* means. "Kids, you mean? Your kids?"

Ethan shrugs. "Someday. But also, Gran needs to stop working so hard, and we can't do that until the debt gets paid off. So, I was wondering how we can collaborate, if there's anything we can do together that would be good for both our farms."

I stare at Ethan. Sure, I have plans for Udderly Creamy, but never in my wildest dreams did I consider my brother might want to work together.

Therefore, nothing comes immediately to mind for a partnership. Nothing except...

"We need more space," I say.

"Who does? Where? For what?"

I shake my head to straighten my thoughts. "In general, at Udderly. A lot of farms do community outreach programs and farm tours, but we don't have a parking lot to accommodate that kind of thing. Plus, you need public bathrooms, literature, and safety equipment. There's extra liability, too."

Ethan rubs his chin. "How can we help with that?"

"Well…I'm not sure yet."

Ethan and I poke and prod at a few ideas, but nothing really solidifies.

"Let me talk to my team," I say.

He grins. "Right, you have a team. I have family, and you have a team." Ethan winces as soon as the words are out of his mouth. "I didn't mean it like that. Sorry. I meant that Bedd Fellows never had farm hands, and I've been leaning on the family to help. You've got a crew that helps you."

"I know what you meant," I mumble. It still stings, though, this proof from the horse's mouth that I'm on the outside looking in.

Our food comes, interrupting the awkwardness, and Ethan switches the topic. "I guess your crew includes Molly."

"Yes." I tuck into the hash browns first while they're hot and crispy.

"How's she working out?" He asks before biting into his Reuben sandwich.

"Good."

"She told us she made a bet with you about your milk sales last weekend."

I almost miss my mouth with the next forkful of potatoes. "Yeah?"

Ethan looks smug. "She wouldn't tell us what you wagered, though."

My face goes beet-red, and my brother laughs.

CHAPTER 18
MOLLY

Wednesday morning, I get a text from an unknown number.

> Come up to the house for lunch.
>
> Alex wants us all together.
>
> Also, this is Kit.

MOLLY

> Did you get my number from Alex because you're too lazy to come down?

KIT

> Maybe…

At one, I trudge up the hill to the big house. I'm the last to come in, and the guys make room for me at the table across from Alex.

I haven't seen him since Sunday night, and we exchange tentative smiles. Kissing him was stupid. I won fair and square, and instead of letting myself off the hook for my impulsive bet, I doubled down. Several times I've caught myself fantasizing about the soft brush of his beard against my chin and have to smack myself for thinking about my boss like that.

Being around the rest of Alex's staff, though, prevents me from blurting out any idiotic questions.

Lunch is some sort of shredded, aromatic pork with stewed beans, rice, and veggies. One of these days, I'm going to have to meet Anna and give her a big 'ole hug.

Kit's telling a story about one of his friends back in Here that has everyone laughing. Alex asks about Luis, Jesús's son, who's graduating high school next month. It's very familiar and warm.

After we eat, though, Alex stacks our empty plates and rests his forearms on the table. "I wanted to ask if anyone has any improvements or suggestions they'd like to make around here."

The table's quiet as the men all exchange glances.

"You can think about it, of course, but I'm game for anything. If there's something you think would be good for the farm, whether that's you or our animals, I want to hear it."

Jesús and Perry offer a few ideas about things I don't frankly understand: homogenizers, cow collars, and corn silage.

Alex takes notes.

"The farm shop could use a little…" I waggle my head, trying to think of a polite way to phrase it.

"Sprucing up?" Alex suggests.

"Gutting and rebuilding?" Kit one-ups.

"Somewhere in between," I say. "It's cute, but it's clothes-heavy. I think some smaller things like stickers or coffee mugs might do better. And, sorry, but the wire racks should go."

Heads nod in agreement. Quiet descends, and we think some more.

Perry rubs his chin. "Why do you ask, boss?"

"Yesterday, my brother asked if there was a way that our

farms could partner together. But I honestly…" Alex rubs his face. "Everything I can think of that I want is new equipment or impossible."

"What's on the list that's impossible?" Kit asks.

"I'd love to give farm tours. There are educational programs we could run here, but we don't have the space. We can't just make space happen. And I'm not sure how that would benefit Bedd Fellows."

The guys go quiet, thinking.

Jesús speaks up. "The best thing for our bottom line is to sell more milk directly, right, boss?"

"Yeah." Alex glances at me and Kit. "The cooperative takes most of our milk, but they pay us way less than the public does."

"Cutting out the middleman," I say.

"Exactly."

"Is strawberry milk just as profitable?"

Kit grins, and Alex rolls his eyes. "More profitable."

"You know, people love strawberry milk. What if we offered it in the farm shop and in the CSA? Maybe even call it a limited run and see how it goes."

"If Ethan has enough strawberries."

"Ugh." Alex puts his head in his hands. "I hate that stuff."

There are snickers around the table.

"Why?" I ask.

"Our stance has always been that our milk is healthy. 'Healthy for you, healthy for the cows, and Udderly delicious.' That's always been our motto."

"The health benefits are still there, aren't they? Kids—and adults—that drink strawberry milk are still getting all the protein and calcium and all that good stuff, right?"

"Yes," Alex begrudgingly admits. "But we have to clean the bottling machine every time, and that's annoying."

"We have to clean it every time anyway," Jesús points out.

"Actually," I muse. "What if we added chocolate milk?"

Alex glares.

"Look, people *love* the strawberry milk. You get tagged on Instagram every weekend by people raving about the milk."

"We do?"

"Yeah. Who runs your social media?"

"Uh. Me." Alex shrugs, chagrinned. Then I see it hit him. "Is this how you knew you could sell enough last weekend?"

"Hell yeah. And now I'm taking over your social media."

"Good riddance," Alex mutters.

"So, call Ethan and ask how many strawberries he can set aside for syrup. We'll email your CSA newsletter—you have one, right?—and offer a limited run of strawberry milk."

"Damn girl," Kit says. "Next thing you know, we'll be calling *you* boss."

"Plus, we should sell strawberries in the farm shop and in the CSA. And Ethel's jam." Okay, now I'm rolling. "Offer everything in the CSA, not just eggs and dairy. Are there any other farmers you know you could work with?"

Alex considers this. "It's not a bad idea. We're one of the more established membership programs in the area, and it would be convenient for the customers, too."

"Is there not a farmer's market nearby?"

"The closest one is Albany. It's not terribly far, but there are other dairies that go. And in the past, it hasn't been great sales for us."

Perry clears his throat. "To be fair, boss, you and I weren't the best at running a stall."

Everyone looks at me. Kit points between me and him. "*We'd* be great at a farmer's market. *You,*" he points between the rest of them, "not so much."

"Be that as it may," Alex says with only a hint of the exasperation he must be feeling, "Molly's leaving at the end of the summer, and you'll be gone before then. Probably. Hopefully."

Alex's eyebrow wiggles, and Kit laughs.

"Okay, so far, the best plan is to sell more strawberries. I'm going to call my brother and inform him of our big plan." Alex's voice has this little lilt to it, a slight tease. It's adorable.

We split up to get back to work.

Down at the farm shop, I pull up pictures of Rose Apothecary from Schitt's Creek. It would be really fun to spruce this place up, but Rose Apothecary relies on antique hutches and white, clean shelving.

Well, it might be a total crapshoot to look for antique hutches, but a nice white shelf system would be easy.

Maybe.

I lose myself in a Pinterest rabbit hole and come out the other side with a plan.

CHAPTER 19
ALEX

AT THE END OF THE DAY, MOLLY KNOCKS ON MY DOOR. "HEY, boss," she says from the doorway.

Trixie whines from her dog bed in the corner. I look at Molly and raise an eyebrow. "You want her to come say hi?"

She grins. "Yes please."

"Say the word."

Molly doesn't just say "okay," she bends down and taps her thighs and Trixie goes bananas, spinning around, jumping like a pogo stick, and just generally being a derp.

I called my brother after lunch, and he said that he has strawberries out the wazoo—all the strawberries that ripen during the week get frozen or made into jam or—for a lucky few—become Gran's desserts. He'll get back to me with a number for how much syrup Gran thinks she can make.

Molly stands and dusts herself off. She's wearing a jean skirt today and a royal blue tank top that hugs her figure.

And I realize I'm alone with her. Kit's in the house. Perry and Jesús are gone. In fact, Molly should be gone too—it's past six.

My heart—and parts lower—wonder if she's here for another kiss. *Okay, play it cool, Alex.*

"What are you doing here?" I ask, and it comes out gruff instead of hopeful—too gruff. Whoops, I overcorrected.

"I did some digging into a farm shop redesign. I think if we can provide the labor ourselves, I can make some improvements."

She shows me pictures on her phone of what she has in mind and drawings she made sketching out the space. It would get rid of all the wire racks, but add in a waist-high counter around most of the room, bracketed shelves, and angled wooden display boxes. She's even drawn out how to use existing reach-in coolers in frames to make them fit the aesthetic.

"How did you do all this?"

"Never underestimate the power of a woman with Pinterest."

I look at the budget she's written out. "What's this number?"

She tilts her head, looking down at the paper. "That's the estimated supplies, assuming we have tools and labor, plus a 15% cushion and rounded up."

I hand her back the paper. It's a good plan. I wish I had time to help her, but I know someone who would love to spend time with her and is antsy to do stuff with his hands. "Deal. You can have Kit—he's handy—and he can drive my truck to get supplies. I have an account at Feed 'n Seed, but there's a bigger hardware store up in Albany."

"Sweet!" Molly bounces on her toes. "Okay, I'm going to plan. And talk to Kit. Oh, and run my ideas by Ethel, too. And I bet my dad would have ideas..."

Molly's barely even with me anymore, so excited and wrapped up in her plans. I can't help but grin down at my laptop while Molly walks away, talking to herself about the shop.

I drop off two ice chests at Bedd Fellows Farms each day of the strawberry picking. And this time, I pay attention to our Instagram account. Someone even posts a photo with Molly in it, and both she and the kid she's posing with have strawberries painted on their faces. My brother must have found an artist to add to the festivities. These events keep getting bigger.

Molly's right about the social media. I need someone to take it over.

Not for the first time, I wish Molly wasn't leaving. I wish she wasn't just passing through Fork Lick. She's a great addition to my staff, and I'll miss seeing her around the farm.

And a chance for another kiss.

I shake the thought out of my head. We still have her for a month. No use crying over milk that hasn't even spilled yet.

Sunday evening, I pull into the Bedd Fellows driveway. Kit stayed home tonight, so it's just me. Trixie goes snuffing, and I climb the front stairs. I can hear my family inside, laughter and conversation ringing out like a beacon.

Everyone says hi, and my stomach gurgles at Gran's cooking, but we sit down at the table, and Molly's still not here. There's not a place set for her.

"Where's Molly?"

"She has book club tonight," Gran says. "Didn't she tell you?"

"No." The word is petulant like I'm a child who had a playdate canceled.

Gran waves my tone away. "You'll bring her a plate after we're done."

Okay, it's less fun without Molly there, but I enjoy myself a lot more than I thought I would without either her or Kit as a buffer. Ethan's in an excellent mood, and after our conversation last week, I'm feeling a lot better, too.

Lighter.

I should have let go of my anger with Grandad a long time ago.

After dinner, I walk a plate of food out to Vaniel. The door is closed, but the windows are open, screens in place to keep the bugs out. I can hear Molly laughing.

Maybe laughing isn't the right word. She's *cackling*.

I look down at the plate and wonder if I should take it back inside and drive Trixie and me home, but I want to see her. Plus, Gran told me to bring the plate to Molly and while I'm okay with turning down an invitation to dinner, I won't outright *disobey* the woman that raised me.

I knock on the door, and Molly tells someone she'll be right back.

Vaniel's door swings open and Molly's backlit by her van's lights.

"Alex," she says, surprised and maybe pleased to see me.

"Here," I say, offering her the plate.

"Oh, thank you. Can you wait just a few minutes? We're almost done, and we could talk while I eat?"

"Sure." I gesture to the two Adirondack chairs outside the van. There's a fire pit, too, but it's too warm to light it. "I'll wait out here."

"Okay," she says, and I can see her megawatt smile within the shadows on her face.

CHAPTER 20
MOLLY

"Who was that?" Natasha asks coyly.

Alex is right outside my door. He can't hear my friends, but he can definitely hear me. I decide to tease. "That was my *friend*," I say. "He brought me dinner." I bat my eyelashes at my book club.

Natasha, Misty, and Chrissy watch me from my computer screen. Misty is a friend from back home, while Natasha and Chrissy are fellow vanlifers I met this year. We all have the same tastes in books, so we read a book once a month together.

There's a chorus of ooooooooooos.

"A friend, as in Alex? Your boss? The one you kissed?" Natasha clarifies.

"Yes, that friend."

They know pretty much everything that's been going on here in Fork Lick. We don't talk about the book we're reading until our call, but we have a group text where I've spilled all the beans.

Unfortunately for Alex, we're still talking about the sex scenes in the book, so when we get back to the subject at hand, the next thing I say to my friends is, "Of course the elf king is going to be dynamite in bed; he's over a thousand years old. If you don't know how to properly eat a woman out by then, you're doing something wrong."

Outside the van, Alex clears his throat. I cover my mouth and giggle.

"You know," I say, leaning forward and comically stroking my chin. "Something I didn't love about this book was the mutual pining."

"Oh, can Alex hear you right now?" Chrissy asks, and I nod.

"Mutual pining can be *so tedious.* You like each other, we get it. Talk it out. Or better yet, bang it out. I love a hero who tells the heroine exactly what he wants. It's so sexy."

My friends are snickering. I'm serious, of course, mutual pining is one of my least favorite set ups because so often I just want to grab the characters and say "kiss" while smooshing their faces together like I used to do with Ken and Barbie.

What's hilarious is that the book we discussed tonight is totally an insta-love, super-fast burn book. There is absolutely zero mutual pining in sight.

Our chat is pretty much over at that point, and I'm very aware that Alex is waiting for me outside, so it's time to go. I say goodbye and blow my friends kisses.

Closing my laptop, I unplug it and push the power cord out the window so I can properly shut the screen. I stand up, stretch, and wonder whether Alex left to give me some privacy or if he's still outside.

My question gets answered real quick when I open the door and step out of Vaniel. Alex is *right there,* looming over me in the darkness. His hand finds my waist, and he gently pushes me against the side of my van. My heart goes wild looking up into the intensity in his eyes.

He bends down, and I close my eyes. Instead of a kiss, though, there's a slight brush of my cheek with his nose, his breath against my mouth, Alex's desires right up against the line, waiting for me to invite him over.

I grab his shirt—a soft flannel—and pull him to me.

Our lips meet in a scorching kiss.

Alex surrounds me, big and warm yet gentle. Our tongues meet, and I cling to him, weak in the knees with the full brunt of his focus. His arms come around me, gathering and stretching me up to my tiptoes to meet him. I slide my hands up from his chest to his shoulders, gripping those hard, hay-bale-tossing muscles underneath my hands before circling his neck.

I moan into his mouth, and he answers with a groan. One of his hands wanders down to my ass and picks me up. The other hand is in my hair, which I wore down tonight, and braces us against the side of Vaniel.

Between my legs, Alex is hard.

My vibrator, which I've been using more and more frequently, really hasn't been cutting it. I blame that for my urgency.

I'm just craving someone else's touch, someone else's warmth. That's why I need it so badly.

That's why I drag my hand down Alex's body and grip his cock through his jeans.

Alex *growls*. It's low and feral, and my whole body clenches. God, I want him.

But a noise breaks through my foggy brain—voices. Alex hears it the same time I do; in one smooth move, my feet are back on the ground. He wipes his face and adjusts himself in his jeans. I straighten my shirt and fix my hair.

The voices are Ethan and Lia walking back to their cabin. One of them shushes the other, and I distinctly hear Alex's name.

"I should go."

I look up at Alex. His voice is rough and gravelly.

"Okay," I agree. Dinner's waiting for me, and nearly getting busted by Alex's family is a wake-up call. I'm mixing family dynamics I don't understand and putting both my jobs on the line. I'm glad that Alex came to dinner without me having to ask him, and I don't want to get between him and his family's delicate relationship, even if it does seem to be improving.

"See you tomorrow."

"See you tomorrow," I echo, and Alex walks off into the night.

CHAPTER 21
ALEX

I'm not avoiding Molly, per se. Kissing her was probably not the right move, but hearing Molly call me *that friend* means she'd told her book club about me. Plus, her talking about sex and pining felt like a hint that I took advantage of.

It was a hint, right?

Either way, it was dumb for me to kiss her. Our first kiss was something sweet that could have been brushed off. But this one cannot be ignored. It was too smoking hot and too inappropriate.

I'm up at the hilltop, and she's down in the farm shop.

I'm her boss, she's my employee.

But instead of being decisive and firm, I avoid the topic entirely by working late, which is nothing new. At least I have a good excuse; I have to spend some time figuring out how to add strawberry milk to our online store so that the CSA customers can place their orders. It's been a while since I've added a new product.

Then it's the same story with our newsletter, which I draft and meticulously check for typos and then send a preview to Colleen, who, even though she teaches children who can't write yet, is a better writer than I am.

I should probably turn this over to Molly or Kit, but then I wouldn't have an excuse to hide in my office, would I?

I run out of excuses on Thursday, though. After breakfast, Kit said he had something to do, so I'm doing chores all on my own this morning. It sure is quieter without Kit, and despite years of doing my chores in silence, I miss his chatter.

After walking through the calf hutches, I head toward the gentle lowing of the cows in the milking robot. Trixie follows at my heel but nudges me before I take the first step into the building.

I look down at her. She stares back up at me.

Hmm.

I glance around, back to the barn, then run my eyes along as much of the pastures as I can see. Nothing seems amiss until my eyes land on the farm shop.

Molly shouldn't even be here yet, so it makes no sense that I see movement. It makes even less sense that I see Ethan's truck parked out front. I stride down the driveway, and when I get close enough, I recognize that Molly, Ethan, and Kit are all down there, moving a bunch of white objects from Ethan's truck into the farm shop.

The first to spot me is Kit, who gives me a big grin, totally unrepentant about whatever he's up to. Then Ethan comes out and ignores my flummoxed expression with a head nod. Lastly, Molly comes out, and when she sees me, her cheeks, already pink from exertion, flush a deeper shade of red, and she smiles.

I have to force my mouth down into a frown so I don't smile like a goober in front of my brother. "What's this?"

Molly puts her hands on her hips, eyes narrowing at my frown. "The farm shop redesign. You told me I could have Kit." Her chin tilts up a little in defiance.

I did. I suppose she's suckered Ethan into free labor, too. The white things they are moving are freshly painted wooden shelves and the large structures that are going to contain the coolers. They've even got decorative vent covers in the front. It looks fancy.

"You already built and painted everything?"

I tell myself it's fine that she didn't need my help. I was too busy anyway.

"We did it at Bedd Fellows in the pole barn since there's space."

"Fair enough."

Ethan and Kit exchange glances, grinning at each other, and I do *not* want to know what that's about.

At my feet, Trixie whines.

The four of us look down at her. Usually, when we come down to the farm stand and the flat lower fields, I let her get some exercise, so I suppose she's Pavlov-dogging it to stretch her legs. Hell, maybe she's been training me.

Or, I realize, maybe her nudge to get me to go down just a few minutes ago was self-serving.

Either way, I suppose I should let her go. "Alright, girl, go long."

Trixie rockets off so fast that she leaves her brains behind. Molly gasps when Trixie leaps through the fence at top speed, but fortunately, this time, she doesn't whack her noggin'—it's happened a handful of times before. Instead, she runs like a bat out of hell. When she does this, her ass tucks down, and her hind legs fly out like she's in position to scoot her butt across the carpet with a case of the worms, but it's just the zoomies.

We line up at the fence to watch her go, Molly next to me, then Kit, then Ethan. Trixie loops around chicken coops in the flat field a few times, tongue lolling and happy as all get out.

"That's the smartest dumb dog I've ever met," Ethan states.

"That's the dumbest smart dog I've ever met," Kit agrees.

The cows, as usual, ignore the dog.

"Easy there," Ethan mutters as Trixie starts up the hill and then thinks the better of it. On the way back down, as expected, momentum gets the best of her, and she tumbles. It doesn't slow her down too much though; she's back up like a flash and shaking it off.

From the side of my eye, I take in Molly. She's dressed for work, jean shorts, sneakers, and a cotton tank top with a sports bra underneath. Her hair's up in a bun, wisps sticking to her face. She's beautiful, as always, but her skin is a little pale, her smile a little tired.

A few more loops around the grass, and Trixie starts to flag. She aims for us again and leaps back out, skidding on the grass and looping back around to flop at my feet, belly up, tongue thick and hanging out of her mouth and acquiring grass flair.

I bend down, placing my hand on the center of her chest. "Good girl," I say. Her heart beats wild under my palm, and the soft hair on her belly is silky and smooth.

On Trixie's other side, Molly bends down, too. Just when I thought Trixie couldn't get any happier, Molly's smaller hand rests on Trixie's chest, just above mine where Trixie's fur does one of those undignified swirls. Molly's thumb strokes softly, and she coos. "What a good girl you are."

Our eyes meet over the supine, panting canine, and Molly smiles at me. This close, I can see that fleck of green again, the tiny mole she has just above her left temple—little details that I tuck away to think about later.

Gently, Molly's finger brushes against one of mine, and heat shoots straight to my crotch.

I straighten up before I get a boner. "Well, I've got more to do back up at the barn." Trixie ungracefully jerks onto her haunches and leans against my calf again.

"Let me walk with you a minute," Ethan says, and together we start up the hill.

"Something you want to talk about?" I ask when we've gotten halfway up the driveway.

"I know Molly's a grown woman who can take care of herself," my brother starts, and I tense. Is he going to tell me to leave her alone? Is he worried about me taking advantage of her? "She's working herself to the bone, though. Gran's worried. Molly works at your place during the week and mine on the weekends. Plus, she comes up to the house on Wednesdays and works alongside Colleen at the kitchen table, and now she's putting in extra work renovating your farm shop."

I grunt. Molly shouldn't have had to work outside the shop hours, but I guess I didn't think that part through. I could have told her to shut the shop down for a day or two, but I was too busy avoiding her like an idiot. And now my brother's noticed the same thing I did—that Molly looks tired—but he's actually doing something about it.

"I'll make sure she gets paid for her extra time," I say.

"If I had more people, I'd offer her a day off, but I don't really have anyone to spare."

That's easier to solve. Imara, my weekend employee who's still in high school, is off for the summer, so I'll ask her if she can come to work. "I'll give her some time off here. If she wants it."

It'll be a start to taking care of Molly.

CHAPTER 22
MOLLY

OF COURSE, THE FARM SHOP ISN'T FULLY FUNCTIONAL WHEN IT opens at nine, but it's close. Ethan came last night after the shop closed to help me take down the wire racks and fill the holes in the wall. I spend the morning selling milk and eggs, refolding and organizing the rest of the merchandise, and doing my best to hide my yawns from customers.

I have more ideas for Alex, but thinking about them makes me sad. I won't be around to make changes or see the farm's success. That goes for both Udderly Creamy and Bedd Fellows.

When one o'clock rolls around, it's not Kit who brings me lunch, but Alex, and my heart does a completely unnecessary flutter when he opens the door, balancing two plates on one arm.

It's nerves, obviously. He's seeing the newly redesigned farm shop for the first time.

I spread my arms wide and grin. "What do you think?"

Trixie follows inside and immediately races around the room, sniffing at the new stuff.

Alex looks around. I added a few touches that Ethel and I picked up from an antique store to make the shop cozier; there's a collection of glass bottles of varying sizes, a few prints of farm life on the walls, and Ethan went through one of his storage sheds and found a bunch of old farm stuff that I've hung on the wall.

"It looks real good, Molly."

My entire body warms at his approval. I haven't seen him since Sunday, but I sure have thought about him a lot. That kiss was something else, and I want to do it again. And again. And again.

But first.

"Good. Now—" I make grabby hands at the plate of food that smells so goddamn amazing, "—gimme."

Alex sets the two plates on the counter, and we unwrap them together, a column of steam rising from them. Underneath, it looks like a quesadilla, but it's crispy. I spot refried beans and cheese and lettuce inside.

It's not cut up, so I follow Alex's lead and pick the whole dang thing up and take a bite out of it.

I moan, and Alex does too. After I swallow, I catch his eye across the counter. "Anna needs to open a restaurant."

"I tell her that all the time. She doesn't want to work that hard while her kids are still around, and she says it would be hard to get the right ingredients in bulk."

"Are there any Mexican restaurants around? In Albany?"

Alex shrugs. "Some. Not the same, though. Burritos or weird fusion." He tells me about a place in Albany called Bombers that closed after twenty-something years and another one in Troy where they served Mexican-Irish fusion. "Not any place that does Oaxacan food like Anna does."

"I want to meet her."

"You will, I'm sure."

"Someday, someday," I tease. "Like someday you'll show me your digester and solar panels?"

"Anytime."

I swallow the last bite of my lunch and dust my hands off.

Anytime better come soon, really, because my time here is almost halfway done.

Trixie whines, and I realize something. "Oh no, her doggie bed." I stashed it in a box in the storage room while we were moving everything. I retrieve it and place it back into the corner where it used to be, and Trixie thanks me with a butt wiggle and a contented sign when she flops down on the bed.

Alex wipes his mouth with his napkin and clears his throat. "Do you needed to take some time off? You've been working a lot between here and Bedd Fellows. And high school is over now, so Imara can come to work."

I think about that for a moment. I have been working a lot, and I'm pretty sure when I get home tonight, I'm going to eat a sandwich and go straight to bed.

But...I know I'm going to owe Quinn several thousand dollars soon. I waggle my head, thinking, while Alex stacks our plates and silverware.

"Okay," I relent. Alex smiles so fast I just catch the flash of teeth before it disappears.

He straightens from the counter and thumps a fist on it. "Good." He doesn't leave, though. Instead, he traces an invisible line on the counter and clears his throat again. His cheeks are pink.

Adorable.

I come around, and Alex shuffles out of the way while I move the plates to give myself room. Then, I hop onto the top of the counter. Alex's eyes darken, and I reach out, grabbing the front of his shirt and pulling him in for a kiss.

Our mouths open immediately and Alex slots right in between my knees, his hands resting gently on my hips. His lips are warm and firm, and we play with each other, a real long, uninterrupted kiss where I get to figure out if he likes a bit of teeth and the sounds he makes when I suck on his tongue.

The counter gives me a few more inches, but I'm still not

level with him. I wrap my calves around his thighs and pull him closer. One of his hands drops to my bare thigh, and he squeezes the muscle under his palm and increases our pace, more urgent and less careful now.

I like this Alex, the one that doesn't have to be a gentle giant. He's careful in everything he does, from petting baby goats to measuring his words, but right now, I feel all that control slipping. It comes for me in a tightening grip and teeth and—

There's a knock on the window, and we rip apart, turning our heads to see who's caught us.

Kit stands in the window, one hand shading his eyes as he peers in and his gaped mouth morphing into a knowing smirk.

He pulls back, pointing at us with both hands and mouthing something.

"What'd he say?" I ask.

Alex sighs. "I told you so. And now he's going to dance."

Kit pumps his hands and swivels his hips, repeating those words over and over again.

Then he shifts, and I cock my head. "Is that the Fresh Prince 'Jump on It' dance?"

"Yup. A favorite. Wait for it…"

Kit only gets two rounds of hip thrusting and cowboying done before he starts something definitely not suitable for young audiences.

I feel Alex's laugh all over—in my knees still pressed to his side and my palms on his chest. I want more and bury my face in the soft cotton of his shirt.

This causes Alex to shout, "Kit! You're embarrassing her."

A moment later, the door opens, and Kit says, "Awe, I was just teasing."

I turn my head toward him so he can see that I'm laughing. His concern vanishes from his face.

"Is there a reason you came down?" Alex asks.

"One of the goats got loose again. Can we steal Trixie? And maybe you too?"

"Yeah."

Kit winks at me before turning around and walking out the door, giving Alex and me a moment alone. Trixie follows him out.

Before he moves, Alex plants a kiss on my forehead. It's tender and sweet, and he reaches up to smooth my hair back, too. I could melt right here and be happy.

"Get some good sleep," he says. "I'll see you soon, okay?"

I nod, sure that every chance I get to see him, we'll be doing some more kissing.

CHAPTER 23
ALEX

I FIND MOLLY AT LEAST ONCE A DAY, AND I THINK SHE DOES THE same. Jesús walks in on us kissing in my office before the farm shop opens on Friday morning. I go to Bedd Fellows Farms an hour early on Saturday to help them set up the strawberry picking, and with my help, Molly has time to sneak away for a few more kisses behind Baabara's shed before I go.

Sunday, I walk her home after dinner with my family, and we make out against the side of Vaniel until I'm so hard it hurts, and Kit yells for me to drive him home.

Then Molly gets her Monday off, and I don't see her all day. Tuesday morning is a comedy of errors, with chickens getting loose, Perry accidentally dropping a crate of milk bottles—empty, thank god—and one of the robots malfunctioning for half an hour while I have hundreds of milkers getting impatient. Finally, Kit *allows* me to bring lunch down to Molly, but only because I think he feels sorry for me.

"I had an idea," Molly says after demolishing a plate of Anna's tamales.

Hm. It sounds like that's a distraction from kissing. I must make a disgruntled noise because Molly grins and leans over the counter to give me a quick kiss. Then she pulls out her phone. "I've been following some other farms on Instagram, and I was thinking about all the stuff that's happening at the strawberry picking. Look what I found."

She turns her phone, and I watch a video of a young calf toddling along a green, expansive lawn. It's got a halter on, and what looks like university students keep coming up to hug and pet it.

"It's a new program the school is doing, bringing in emotional support animals to help ease the stress of finals week. But there are a lot of other interactions, too—goat yoga, farmer's markets, retirement communities. You could do something like this."

"Like what, exactly?"

Molly tucks her phone back in her pocket. "Ask Ethan if you can bring a baby cow or two to the strawberry picking. Put them in a little pen and let people pet them. People eat that kind of stuff up."

I rub my chin. That might work. Someone would have to stay with the calves, and we're already a little short-handed on the weekends since Jesús and Perry alternate time off. It's not quite farm tours, but it would help foster conversation about where the strawberry milk—and the regular, healthier kind—comes from.

When I return to the main barn—after almost getting caught by a customer with my hand up Molly's shirt—Perry flags me down.

"One of the milkers is limping. I checked her hoof and didn't see anything, so we might need to call Gavin."

I follow Perry out to the cow that refuses to go down the hill. We encourage her to walk, which she does. It's barely noticeable, but there is a limp. I call Gavin, the farrier in Climax who comes a few times a year to take care of our herd, who says he can come by around six.

By then, Perry and Jesús have gone home, and my night crew is here. Kit and I get the cow into one of the stalls to keep her separated from the herd and stay out of the way. That's where Molly finds us.

I explain that we're waiting on the farrier.

Molly looks at the cow with wide eyes.

"Want to touch her?" Kit asks.

Her face scrunches up. "I dunno. She's big."

"Scared of a cow?" Kit teases.

"Come on, meet Daisy," I say, grabbing her hand and leading her over to the cow's head. Daisy—technically Daisy the ninth or something, because we have a lot of cows and don't get creative, but it's better than calling her 2/31, which is the number on her ear tag—is a brown Swiss, so she's got a soft gray coat and a gentle face. I scratch her forehead, and her ears flick.

I keep rubbing her face while Molly gently touches her neck, flattening her palm along the soft hairs.

After a moment, Daisy lowers her head back down to grab another mouthful of hay. At my nudge, Molly moves farther to Daisy's shoulder and keeps stroking.

Kit clears his throat. "While I have you two here, we need to talk about something."

Molly gasps dramatically. "Are you breaking up with me?"

Instead of laughing, Kit winces. A knot settles somewhere between my heart and my throat.

"I've been talking to my parents, and they need some help with their summer rentals. The cleaning service they usually use raised their rates again and nearly doubled their travel fees."

Kit's parents own a slew of rental cabins in Here, and with summer ramping up it's about to get busy. Unfortunately, there isn't a cleaning service in Here, and they don't have enough rentals to justify hiring someone, nor the business year-round to support it.

"I told my parents I'd come back home and help them out.

Which means…"

"You're leaving," I finish.

"Yeah." Kit's voice is soft, sad.

It echoes my feelings. Having my best friend here for over a month has been the most fun I've had in a long time. I've gotten used to his laughter, his jokes with my staff, and him being the first and last person I see every day.

We clear the few feet between us and hug. It's a long one; a good one. One we only break because I can hear the farrier finally arriving.

When we pull apart, Kit sniffs. "I don't think I'll like cleaning houses with anybody else as much as I like shoveling shit with you."

Molly snort-giggles, and Kit turns and wraps her up in a huge hug while I go greet Gavin. When I return, they're talking quietly by the wall, so I focus my attention on Daisy.

Once I explain what's going on, I leave him to his work, and find Kit and Molly whispering to each other. Kit has a look on his face I recognize: feigned innocence.

"What are you doing?" I ask, already regretting the question.

Molly skips off to talk to the farrier, and Kit hisses "traitor" under his breath as she goes past.

I raise an eyebrow.

"Molly tells me that Gavin is a silver fox."

I look back at the farrier. Yup, I'm jealous of a man who's probably thirty years my senior.

Molly is now taking pictures of him working. "Molly, what are you doing?" I can't decide whether I'm more horrified that she's taking pictures of him or that she thinks he's hot.

"What?" I swear her innocent face is getting more and more like Kit's. "I'm taking pictures for your Instagram account. It shows loving and tender care for Daisy here."

I'm sure the cow is the focus of the pictures, but Molly

grins at me and then blows me a kiss, and my jealousy melts away.

She takes a few more photos and comes back to me. "Are you gonna be much longer?"

"Probably. You could hang up at the house for a bit."

Instead of answering, Molly turns to Kit. "When do you leave?"

"Thursday."

So soon.

Molly stretches to kiss Kit on the cheek. "You two have some fun on your last few nights here. I'll head home. But promise me lunch tomorrow."

"Deal."

CHAPTER 24
MOLLY

OVER THE NEXT WEEK, MY TIME WITH ALEX IS A BIT MORE LONG-comforting-hugs and less hot-can't-keep-our-hands-off-each-other make-out sessions. Alex is grumpier than usual, more closed off, and less quick to smile at my jokes.

I see him every morning, either at Udderly Creamy or when he drops off milk at Bedd Fellows, and every evening before I leave work or when he picks up empty ice chests. Alex made sure I took a day off last week, but who's making sure he takes a day off?

Now that Kit's gone, I can clearly see what I only got hints of before—Alex is lonely.

He's got his farmhands, but now he has Sunday dinners with his family and his time with me—for only a few more weeks.

Quinn wraps up the battery replacement. When I come home to Vaniel on Saturday, she is almost done, and with a few flips of switches, my van powers up again. We run the engine for a bit to make sure the alternator is charging the batteries and even test my electric kettle.

I hold my breath when I plug in my laptop, knowing that if anything is going to get fried, my computer would be the worst possible thing. I don't think Quinn notices the quiet exhale of relief.

Wednesday, I'm at the farm shop. Now that I've paid Quinn for her work—a good chunk out of my bank account—I'm working to save up for the next leg of my trip.

Unfortunately, though, I'm having a snafu, and it's one of my own making.

My eczema is bothering me—really bad. There's no one to blame but myself.

First of all, my rashes come in flare-ups—I'm not sure what triggers them. When they come on, I try to treat them as best that I can, but I never medicate for as long as I should. It's not enough that the rash is *mostly* gone.

You'd think I would know better by now. Instead, I have these moments at night when I lay in bed, realizing I didn't put on my ointment and gloves or the bandage on my wrist, depending on which spot is flaring up. In the dark, though, I'm lazy. I justify myself by saying it's not *that* bad and I'll take care of it tomorrow.

It is that bad, and I won't.

It's frustrating that I don't take better care of myself, and it makes me think of my dad. I'm always on him about taking his meds and keeping an eye on his prosthetic, but I don't take care of myself?

Ugh.

So here I am, counting down until I can go home at six. Of course, I want to say goodbye to Alex, but I won't linger. My skin is itchy and stinging, and I've got to get home and put on the heavy-duty ointment.

I call Alex to see if he'll swing by the shop so I don't have to go up to the barn, but he doesn't answer.

Time passes. I tap my nail on the counter for the fiftieth time and check my phone for the tenth. No response. He's probably doing something superbly adorable, like bottle-feeding a goat or giving a cow a good head scratch.

Finally, it's six. I'll go find him.

I lock the shop up before I trudge up the driveway. At the top, I have to stop to "admire the view"—aka catch my breath —before I enter the barn and roam through the building. It's quiet save for the lowing of cows and bleating of goats.

His truck is still here, so I know he's around somewhere.

Exiting the barn, I look out over the view again—rolling hills in shades of green, cloud-spotted, bright blue sky. We just had the summer solstice, and the days are getting shorter. It won't be long before fall colors are on us, and the view from the farm will move from beautiful to drop-dead gorgeous.

Movement catches my eye. There he is. Alex's familiar shape is down at the bottom of the paddock with someone else, the far paddock that you can't quite see from the shop. There's a truck backed up to where they stand with the tail-gate down.

The field is empty of animals, so I let myself in the gate at the top and start down the hill. I can talk to Alex, exit the far gate, walk back to the shop, and get my bike to ride out. I'll be home in no time.

"Alex," I call down, cupping my hands around my mouth. Alex looks up, and it's too far to tell for sure, but I swear he smiles at me. It's good progress—getting Alex to smile instead of frown is like trying to break a habit.

I take long strides down the slope. Ethel recently told me over a shared breakfast that this is a hot spot for sledding in the winter, and I can believe it. It's steep but grassy, and with a few inches of snow, it's a wintery playground.

About fifty feet from Alex, he turns to look at me. Perry is the other man with him, and they're leaning against the fence, real casual, though lord knows what they are talking about here, especially when Alex has a perfectly good office.

My gaze meets Alex's, and for a moment, I think I am going to get a smile. But just as quickly as it appears, it's gone, and concern flashes on his face. "Molly, watch out!"

I spin around, thinking maybe a cow is in the pasture and gunning for me, but I don't even have time to process before my foot slips out from under me and I take a one-two hit, ass over teakettle, and land in a sprawling heap on the grass.

And something smells.

CHAPTER 25
ALEX

P ERRY AND I RUSH OVER TO M OLLY. I TRIED TO WARN HER ABOUT the cow patty, but I was too late—just like I was too late remembering that I left my phone in the office despite having told her to track me down before she left.

She stepped right into it, and, unfortunately, her downhill momentum kept her moving even after she hit the ground. Her massive bun of curls came to rest directly in the pile of cow shit.

Perry and I land on either side of her.

"Are you okay?" he asks first, brow creased in concern.

"Did you hit your head?" I ask.

Molly's brows match ours. "Yes? And no?"

"Yes, you're okay, and no, you didn't hit your head?" I clarify.

"Right. I mean, I kind of did hit my head, but the ground is pretty soft. Or whatever I landed in…" She raises her head slightly, and her arm comes up.

"I…wouldn't do that," I caution her.

Her head falls back with an enormous sigh. "I fell in cow shit, didn't I?"

"That is the bad news."

Her eyes close. "It's all over my hair, isn't it?"

"Yes."

Her throat works as she swallows, and her lower lip trembles slightly.

Aw, hell.

Her eyes still closed, she whispers, "Alex?"

"Yeah?"

She sniffles. "It's in my underwear."

I grab her hand, clasping it in mine. "Hey, sweetheart, it's okay. Come on. Let's get you home so you can get cleaned up."

She pouts, and not the cute pout when she wants to get her way, but the pout of someone who *really* just wants to make her day disappear. "I don't want to bike home with cow shit in my underwear."

"That's fair," I say. "I'll drive you home."

"Then I'll just get your car all dirty."

"Believe me"—I wiggle her hand so her entire arm moves, hoping she'll open her eyes and shake it off—"I've had worse in my car."

That lip trembles again. Fuuuuuuuuuuccccckkkkk.

"Or," I say. "You can shower up at my house."

That gets her eyes open. "But my clothes."

"We'll wash them."

She sighs, but they're clear when she opens her eyes again. Molly wiggles and braces herself against my hand, and Perry and I help her stand. I bend over, looking at her backside, and use the broad side of my hand to knock the worst of the mess off.

"Ew, don't touch that! You're getting all dirty."

"Molly," I say as patiently as I can. "I've had my arm up a cow's ass today. I can handle a little more shit. See if you can shake out your hair a little." I was wearing a glove, obviously, but I don't mention that.

Molly grimaces but does some magic to release her hair from her bun to shake it out. It's not much help, truth be told, but she stands a little straighter, so at least it got better in her mind.

We bid Perry goodbye. He gets back to work welding, trying to finish the job before he goes home, and with my hand under Molly's elbow, I help her climb back up the hill toward my house.

At my back porch, Trixie greets us, her sniffer going wild, her tail even wilder. Molly and I toe off our shoes in the mudroom.

Molly stands, arms slightly held out, and looks around. "Should I just strip here so I don't track shit throughout your house?"

I grunt. "No. You're not leaving a trail behind, so I think it's best if you just go directly into the shower." I lead the way through my bedroom and into the bathroom, grabbing my hamper as I go. "Put your clothes in the basket. Once I hear the water running, I'll come in and grab the dirty clothes and put some clean ones for you to borrow on the counter." I wave vaguely at the shower stall. "Help yourself to whatever you want. Towels are in that cabinet there." I glance at her. "Need anything?"

She shakes her head.

"I'll be back, and good news: you'll be feeling a hundred percent better."

CHAPTER 26
MOLLY

MORE LIKE A THOUSAND PERCENT BETTER. STRIPPING OFF MY clothes was disquieting. Yes, the cow shit had made it in my underwear. When I slid, my shirt must have ridden up and exposed the back of my pants. The small of my back and the waistband of both my jeans and underwear were filthy.

But after stepping under Alex's shower head, I don't have a care in the world. The water pressure beats down on me, the temperature near scalding—just how I like it, even though it's not good for my skin—and I squirt another glob of shampoo into my palm so I can wash my hair a second time.

There's a knock at the door, and I hear Alex's voice. "Can I grab the clothes?"

"Yeah," I call back. It's kind of comforting to hear Alex move around on the other side of the shower curtain, and I smile to myself when I hear him tell Trixie to "back up."

"I left some clothes on the counter for you. I'm going to shower upstairs, and then I'll start the laundry."

"Thank you."

The door closes again. I rinse the shampoo out and use Alex's body wash and his loofah to scrub my skin, thoroughly soaping the small of my back. It stings my hands slightly, but I'd rather be clean.

Before coming to Udderly Creamy, I'd thought cow patties were solid and flat, like a Frisbee. But if you hang around cows even a little, you see firsthand that cow patties are only that way because they've dried out in the sun. I must have stepped right into a very fresh pile.

When finished, I step out of the shower and grab two towels from the cabinet. I wrap my hair with one towel and then grab the second to dry my skin.

Alex has set a stack of clothes on the sink—the "hers" side of the double vanity. There are several options: tee-shirts, sweatpants, boxers, and a flannel shirt. I try the sweatpants first, but they're insanely long on my short legs. The boxers fit better, and I roll the waistband so they don't hang to my knees. The material is soft and terracotta-colored.

The tee-shirt would fit, I'm sure, but the flannel, a dark blue, is so comfortable-looking I can't help but slide it over my shoulders and snuggle into it. It smells clean but also slightly like Alex—like grass and hay and warm animals and something deep and earthy.

Finally, there's a pair of socks. They're cotton and way too big for me, but I slip them on anyway, the heel riding up past my ankle.

I look ridiculous, but as soon as I step out of the bathroom, the thought completely vanishes from my mind because I'm in Alex's bedroom and my gaze lands immediately on something I was too distraught to notice before.

Trixie has a fucking canopy bed. And it's pink.

It's got a frame that raises the bed off the floor, and on top of that, there's a giant fluffy pink dog bed with raised sides and a sunken middle. I think it's memory foam. The wooden legs of the bed continue up to the canopy, which is flat and encloses the bed on three sides, like a little box. The bed looks well-used, the fabric a little pilled and covered in dog hair.

"Adorable," I say to myself. Then, I take a moment to look around the rest of the room. The bed is tidy, and the comforter is smooth. I wonder if Alex makes it every morning or if he made it while I was in the shower. There's a bedside lamp on, even though it's still fairly light out. His bedding is solid navy, the frame a sturdy pine. Very manly.

I turn to the door, and my eye catches on a framed photograph on his dresser. I step closer and lean in. There are five kids and a couple sitting on the stairs to Ethel's front porch. The man—Alex's dad, I assume—sits a step above his mom, and she leans an elbow on his knee. He's smiling right at the camera, and while she's also smiling, she's looking at the side where her children are as if keeping tabs on them.

It's easy to spot Alex. He's frowning, almost pouting at the camera. Ethan has the same smile he does now, and they look almost the same age, even though I know Alex is a year younger.

Colleen has a sweet smile on her face, and I guess that it's Sam, her twin, sitting right next to her. Jackson, the youngest, looks like he's up to no good. I wonder what happened immediately after the photo—or before, for that matter. It's no small feat to wrangle five children who look to be under the age of ten.

I'll ask Ethel if she took the photo. For now, though, I straighten up and head toward the kitchen, following the sounds Alex is making.

Alex's bedroom is just off the living room, which leads to the dining room, where I've had lunch with the guys, and then into the kitchen. Trixie spots me first, her tail thumping on the cabinets as she runs to greet me. Alex looks up from the stove, a smile freezing on his face when he catches sight of me. His eyes drift down, taking me in from the towel on my head to the oversized flannel I've barely buttoned to the socks on my feet that keep my toes off the chilly stone floor.

He's wearing a tee-shirt and pajama pants like the ones that were too long for me. They look good on him, and I've never seen him in anything other than jeans. This is at-home, comfortable Alex.

"Hi," I say, very aware that I'm wearing his clothes in his house. While I should feel ridiculous in this outfit...I don't—not with the way that Alex looks at me.

The counter closest to me by the stove is empty, so I turn and hoist myself up onto the countertop. This puts me almost eye-level with Alex, and I catch a big whiff of dinner—garlic, acidic tomatoes, and spices. Wordlessly, Alex picks up one of two filled wine glasses and passes it to me.

"Thank you." I lean over and peer into the pan. "What's for dinner?"

"Falafel shakshuka."

"What's that?"

"Middle Eastern dish. Tomatoes, peppers, and eggplants."

I sip my wine and watch as Alex places pre-cooked falafel patties into the simmering tomato sauce, covers the pan, and then pulls bread out of the oven. It's store-bought, unlike the treats Ethel bakes, but it still smells good, and Alex slices it up with a serrated bread knife.

Thinking back over the meals I've shared with Alex, I realize he always takes the vegetable choices. Anna makes something meatless every day. "Are you vegetarian?" I ask.

He shrugs. "Mostly."

I tilt my head. "Is it because you raise animals?"

"I've seen how the sausage is made, so to speak. I realize there are many flaws in the dairy industry, and I don't think I'd eat milk and eggs either, except that I know we treat our animals well. Is that a problem?"

I shake my head.

"When I eat somewhere else, like Gran's, I don't make a big deal out of it. If there's a meatless option, I'll do it."

"You know," I say, spinning the wine in my glass. "Lia has a restrictive diet and Ethel's been really accommodating. I bet if you talked to your grandmother, she'd make sure you don't have to eat meat."

He shrugs again. "It hasn't been an issue before. Either Anna cooks for me, or I cook for myself."

I wasn't aware that Alex cooked. After lunch, we all take a few minutes to pack away leftovers, and I've noticed his fridge is pretty empty. And there are always lunch leftovers.

"Do you cook a lot?"

"Nah," Alex says. He dumps the warm bread into a basket and covers it with a cloth napkin. His gaze darts down to my chest before he glances away. "I mostly eat leftovers."

I tilt my head. "I like seeing this domestic side of you, Alex Bedd."

His eyes dart to me again. I don't think the flush of his cheeks is *entirely* the heat of the stove. Alex's eyes travel up and down my body. "I like every side of you, Molly Perkins."

I turn and place my wine glass down before holding out my hand to him. He takes a step forward so I don't have to tug him, and his hands go to my waist. Then we're kissing, slow and soft, and I can taste the wine on his mouth, feel the slight dampness of his beard and hair from his own shower.

Alex breaks the kiss, but instead of pulling away, he bends down. The flannel has slid off my shoulder, and Alex presses a soft kiss to my clavicle, making me gasp.

When I open my eyes, he's back at the stove, and the air between us is easier. I drink my wine and ask Alex about his day, while he cracks eggs into wells he made in the shakshuka. Four perfect eggs simmer in the pan before he puts the lid back on and turns to me.

"Is your hand okay?"

"What?" I look down and realize I've been rubbing the side of my palm where my rash is. "Oh, damn it. Sorry." I drop my hand and shove it under my thigh. I'd been feeling so sexy, and now my body has ruined it.

CHAPTER 27
ALEX

"No, show me." I tug at Molly's forearm and, reluctantly, she shows me the cracked skin under her pinkie. There are also some dry patches between her fingers and on her wrist bone, though they aren't as red and angry.

"It's eczema," she quickly explains. "Not contagious. I haven't been taking good care of it, and I was looking for you to tell you I was going home so that I could put my medicine on."

I frown, tracing my thumb carefully over the broken skin. "Do you have some in your bag? If it's still down at the farm shop, I can get it for you."

She sighs. "No, the medicine is an ointment, and I have to apply it under band-aids or gloves because it gets everything oily, so I don't carry it with me. I kind of wish I did now, though."

I'm no stranger to cracked and chafed skin. "Hang on, I might have something for you."

I slide open a drawer on Molly's other side, the junk drawer, and pull out a green metal tin. "Try this stuff."

Molly reads the label and then opens it up and smells it. Yeah, okay, it doesn't smell the best, but it's worth it.

"Come 'ere." I scoop a finger into the moisturizer and

carefully slather some of the Bag Balm on her skin. I only intended to hit the trouble spots, but I pulled too much out, and the next thing I know, I'm massaging it into her palms and running my hands down her fingers. My hands are big and rough, working hands. Hers are small, of course, the pads of her fingers soft and the backs of her hands freckled.

When I glance up, Molly's watching me. I've moved closer, her knees on either side of my hips. I desperately want to kiss her again, but the eggs are set, and dinner's ready.

Reluctantly, I break away from Molly. I take the cast-iron skillet off the stove and set it down on potholders on the table. I move our wines and set plates out.

Molly hops off the counter and hands me the tin. "Thank you. It's a little…" She opens and closes her hands, feeling the residue left behind.

"Don't worry about touching anything. I never do and I use this stuff every day in the winter."

She smiles at me. "Okay."

Molly tells me she'll be right back and disappears into my bedroom. When she returns a moment later, she's taken the towel off her head and her damp hair, dark and weighted down by the water, seems longer and straighter. She swings a leg over the bench and sits facing the window, looking out over the view. It's a little after seven, so it's still full daylight out. For a moment, I wish it was sunset, and I had candles to light. That would be romantic as hell.

Not that I own candles. And I've never had dinner with a woman I'm falling for at my dining room table.

The thought makes my footsteps stutter as I carry silverware over. Falling for? Jesus, this is bad. Molly's leaving, and here I am mooning over romantic dinners. We haven't even had sex yet.

But then Molly looks over her shoulder at me, warmth in her gaze and a hint of a teasing smile on her lips, as if she can read my mind. No matter what we have or haven't done, how much time we have left, it doesn't matter at all.

I'm still a goner.

After dinner I send Molly out on the porch with a replenished glass of wine and Trixie at her heels while I do dishes. But the time I dry my hands, the daylight is finally fading, and I snag a blanket before stepping out to join her. "I thought you might get cold."

Molly smiles up at me from her Adirondack chair. "You thought right. However..."

She jumps up, holding her wine glass, and gestures for me to sit. I do, and Molly climbs into my lap, arranging our limbs until she's snug against my chest, the blanket draped over the arm of the chair instead of us.

She hums in contentment. "You're so warm."

We drink our wine and watch the daylight fade. I can hear the animals in the barn, the insects up in the trees, and occasionally, Trixie sighs at our feet. Molly's damp hair is soaking through my shirt, but I couldn't care less.

Here I am again, being sappy. This is the kind of evening a man could get used to. Granted, most nights I don't have Perry staying late and taking care of the animals.

I better put this night to good use. Who knows if I'll get another one before Molly takes off?

I put my wine glass down with a decisive click, and Molly hands me hers, still half full, which I put down next to mine. Briefly, I wonder if we're having the same thoughts because when I reach down for Molly, she's reaching up for me. This kiss is harder and more impatient, and soon, I'm half-turned in the chair, craning over a slumped Molly, her head back against the armrest and my mouth at her throat.

That damn flannel of mine that she's been wearing has

been driving me crazy all night. She buttoned it so low I could see the valley between her breasts. The same valley my lips are working toward right now. From below, my hands slide up her waist, and I cup my palm along her ribs right under her breast. She's burning up here, and I feel the *bum-bum, bum-bum, bum-bum* of her racing heart against my palm.

"Alex," she whispers, and it's breathy with a hint of begging. I don't have enough hands to do everything I want to do: hold her mouth to mine, feel her hair between my fingers, pinch her nipple, slide into the boxers she's wearing and confirm that she's bare underneath. When I'd found her underwear in the pile of clothes, I'd clenched it for a moment, dizzy knowing that Molly had been wearing blue string bikini panties all day.

"Alex." This time it's firmer and accompanied by a tug on my hair. I remove my lips from her skin and look up, loving the glaze of arousal in her eyes. "We are literally two rooms over from your bed. Can we please—"

I stand before she can finish her sentence and scoop her out of the chair. She laughs, and Trixie scrambles to her feet behind us with an excited *woof* because the humans are playing.

When I step into my bedroom, I tell Trixie, "Go to your room," and my dog darts into her bed.

"Oh my god," Molly says. "I forgot to tease you about that. Your dog has a pink—oof!"

I peel back my comforter and drop Molly on my mattress, covering my mouth with hers. Her laugh turns into a moan, and she wraps herself around me. I grab her thigh, flexing my body to grind my hard cock between her legs while continuing our kiss.

Molly's giving as good as she's getting, arching up to rub against me. "Fuck, sweetheart, you feel so good," I mumble between kisses.

"Alex, please, I need you."

Those words shoot straight to my dick, and I rear back, gripping both sides of my flannel and yanking. Buttons—the few that Molly had done up—fly across the room. I place an open-mouthed kiss on one breast and then the other. Molly's outright writhing beneath me. While my mouth works, sucking and nipping, I shove the boxers down Molly's thighs and then smooth a hand down her belly, through her soft curls, and into her wet, slippery cunt.

Molly cries out, and I listen, paying attention to every cry and gasp while I work my fingers inside her, my thumb against her clit, my tongue against her nipple until her body tenses and clamps around my fingers. Her silent scream arches her chest up, and her hands thread into my hair, holding me to her while she comes.

I slow, easing my fingers out and gentling my tongue, until Molly hums in satisfaction.

Pushing up on one hand, I gaze down at her. Her eyes are lidded, and her freckles stand out from her cheeks, which are flushed and plump with a smile.

"Please tell me you have a condom."

"Fuck yeah I do." After our first kiss, I checked my stash and resupplied condoms and lube—something I tried to sneak into a bag of groceries, but Kit found and teased me for.

I sit up, put my fingers in my mouth to clean them off, and then pull my shirt off over my head.

When I can see her again, Molly is chuckling.

"What?"

"You have no idea how sexy you are, do you? Next time you lick your fingers off, make eye contact."

My cheeks heat.

"Actually, make eye contact when you take your shirt off like that, too. It was hot." Her eyes drop over my chest. "Holy hell, Alex, you've been hiding that body under all those flannels?"

I shuck my pants off and crawl over her. "Shut up," I say, but it comes out charmed instead of embarrassed.

We get distracted by kissing for a moment, but then I reach for the bedside table and peel open a condom. Molly watches, her bottom lip dimpled against her teeth while I roll it on and press against her opening.

It takes some repositioning, and I almost reach for the bottle of lube, but then Molly relaxes, and I slide in a few more inches. She hums and softens, and I thrust a few times, building to a rhythm that has her gasping and crying out beneath me.

I'm so overwhelmed by the heat and the sounds she makes that I have to pull back. We both breathe hard, and I push up on my hands to give us some space.

"Okay there?" she pants.

"Gettin' too excited," I admit.

She laughs, and I can feel it around my dick.

When she reaches for me, I lower down to my forearms again. She plants an achingly slow kiss on my lips.

"I like this," she whispers.

"I like you," I whisper back.

Molly's eyes roam over my face, and her fingers run through my hair, over the back of my head, and down to my beard, as if she's petting me.

"Tell me what you like," she says, cocking her head.

"I fucking love your legs." I punctuate it with a thrust. Her eyes dance. "I love your hair." I card my fingers through her curls. When I meet her eyes again, Molly's holding back laughter, and I think back to what I said until it clicks. "Oh, you meant in bed."

"Yeah, but don't stop."

I kiss her teasing mouth, making it a deep one, only pulling back when she's panting for breath and her eyes are hazy.

I take slow drags, pulling in and out of her body. Molly practically purrs.

"You like these legs?" Her knees squeeze my side.

"Yeah." I shift to slide a palm up from her knee to her ass. "I want them wrapped around me."

Molly raises her feet and locks them behind my back. "What else do you want?"

"Anything?" I whisper.

"Anything."

"I want to take you hard and make you scream." I kiss down her throat, thrusting deeper. "I want to spread you out and eat you for breakfast." She digs her heels in, encouraging me to move faster.

"Bent over your desk," she pants.

Jesus. "On a blanket under the stars in my truck bed." My groin tightens, and I pass the point of no return, fucking into her harder. "Right here in my fucking bed." I grunt, coming and straining inside her body, my head thrown back.

Molly strokes her hands up down my arms, quietly letting me come down. When I finally relax and roll off her, she props herself up on her elbow. "Alex Bedd. Who knew you had so much to say?"

I chuckle and roll off the bed to clean up. When I come back, Molly curls into me, asking what we should do next. I have some ideas, and I whisper them in her ear in a low voice, stroking her skin until I get hard again.

And then we do them.

CHAPTER 28
MOLLY

ALEX SHUFFLING AROUND IN THE DARK WAKES ME UP.

"Wha time?" I ask, my face pressed into the pillow and my groggy brain not able to fully form words yet.

A hand cups my head, warm and solid. "Early. Go back to sleep. Anna might be in the kitchen when you wake up."

I fall back asleep.

When I wake up again, the sky outside the window is a soft blue, and noises come from the kitchen. It takes me a moment to remember Alex's words.

I get up and see my clothes from yesterday loosely folded on the dresser. The house is a little chilly, so I forego my tank top. A flannel sounds too good to pass up. I slide my underwear and shorts on and then help myself to a flannel in Alex's closet.

Avoiding the kitchen, I exit the house through the porch and walk toward the barn. There's a slight mist hanging over the fields, and the sun should be up any minute now. One shed is open, a truck backed in, and there's a soft and rhythmic *thump* of movement.

At the open door, I pause and take in the view. Alex has his back to me, picking up bales of hay and stacking them.

The truck bed is half-full, so he's got more work to do…but he's whistling.

It's jaunty and upbeat and I can't help but smile.

"Morning," he says over his shoulder, and my heart melts when I hear the smile in his voice.

"Up for a roll in the hay?"

He picks up another bale. "It's barley."

I laugh and shake my head just as an actual cowbell rings out from the house. Behind me, I hear a door shut.

"I'll be up for breakfast in a minute," Alex says.

"Okay. See you then."

I walk back to the house and take the front door this time, toeing my shoes off and adding them to the collection. Turning the corner, I spot Jesús already at the table and a short, heavy-set woman who must be Anna.

Her mouth rounds when she spots me.

"Hi, Anna." I offer her my hand. "I'm Molly."

Her gaze darts over my face and behind her, Jesús coughs. Anna bats my hand away and pulls me in for a hug. "Dios mio. I've heard so much about you."

"Your food is so good. I've been dying to meet you."

Anna's gaze darts to the top of my head before meeting my eyes again. She blinks like she's trying to remember what I said. Something feels weird.

The door opens behind me, and Alex stomps in. I turn to greet him, and his eyes flicker upward, too. What the hell?

Alex flushes and steps up to me, whispering in my ear. "You may want to fix your hair."

"My—" Reaching up, I feel for the giant bun I usually keep my hair in at the farm…and realize that I did not redo it this morning. My mouth drops in horror when my hand meets an absolute rat's nest of hair.

I dart to the half bath that's by the front door and the view in the mirror makes me gasp. This is beyond rat's nest, beyond fresh-out-of-bed hair. We've hit freshly fucked territory. God, I can practically see the furrows Alex's fingers left in it.

Flipping my head over and snapping the band out, I finger-comb it the best I can and re-do the bun.

Okay. I survey myself in the mirror. Not so bad.

There's a knock on the door and when I crack it, Alex pokes his head in. "You okay?"

"Aside from looking like a hot mess this morning? Sure."

"A beautiful hot mess," he amends, and my insides melt again. Alex steps all the way inside the room and bends down, gently pressing a kiss to my lips. "Good morning, sweetheart."

And what do you know, my outsides melt, too. I'm just a puddle of feelings inside this tiny bathroom with a man who smells like sweat, morning dew, and barley.

The balance in my bank account grows, and the days keep warming up. I spend less and less time in Vaniel, to the point that Alex picks me up and drops me off with the milk every Saturday and Sunday for the strawberry pickings.

I bring my white eczema gloves and ointment with me to his house for our sleepovers. When I put them on at night and make Mickey Mouse jokes, Alex casts me a bemused look and kisses me.

We don't outright say anything to the Bedds, but we spend Sunday night dinner with Alex's hand on my thigh under the table and knowing looks from everyone else.

The clock is ticking, though. I only have a few more weeks left committed to the farm shop, and while we haven't talked about the end of us, he mentioned that one of his former shop managers who is home from college for the summer could pick up some shifts when I leave.

Other changes come, too. Someone named Diane moves

into the house with Ethel. She's a friend of Colleen's, and she and Ethel talk about seeds and plot out Ethel's new raised bed. Over the next week, another van and an RV are parked near Vaniel, but they leave by the weekend. The late-season strawberries dwindle, replaced by blueberries and blueberry milk.

I decide that I'm missing Vaniel. We haven't stayed the night in my van for size reasons, but that doesn't mean I don't want to do something in him.

Actually, thinking about having sex in Vaniel makes me regret ever personifying my van. I'm going to have sex with Alex *inside* Vaniel of the he/him pronouns? Ugh, what am I doing to myself? Not that having sex inside a female van is any better.

Or worse?

Whatever.

When Alex comes by Sunday morning, it's the first time he's setting up the calf pen for petting. He's got a baby cow *in his truck's backseat,* and let me tell you, watching him lift her out and set her on the ground is flipping adorable. He waits for Perry to hop out and take over with the calf before he finds me.

I'm still setting up the tables and buckets, but we meet in the shadows of the pole barn for our usual quick kiss.

"Wait," I say, tugging on Alex's sleeve before he can pull too far away. We're tucked into a corner by the bathroom door, and Alex settles his back against the wall. I reach into the pocket of my shorts and pull out a condom.

Alex's eyes go big when he sees it. "Here? Now?"

I laugh. "No." I slip the condom into the pocket on his pec and pat it. "Just a little reminder for you today. Think of me and then we'll slip away before dinner."

Alex groans, rolling forward to press his forehead against mine. "You kill me, sweetheart."

I smirk and flounce away, leaving Alex to deal with the erection I felt growing against my hip.

I keep an eye on Alex and Perry setting up. We didn't advertise that we were bringing a calf today, hoping to keep expectations low in case it doesn't go well. Eventually, Perry heads back to Udderly, leaving Alex to manage by himself.

We were worried about nothing. It's a hit. They chose the calf, Mootilda, because she's calm and sweet-tempered, and she delivers. Sometimes, she's out of the pen, with Alex holding on to her halter, and sometimes she's in the pen for a break, so the kids can look at her with wonder on their faces and the parents can take pictures when Mootilda sticks her tongue through the wire gaps.

At the end of the day, everyone's in a good mood. Perry swings by to pick up Mootilda, and it's easy for us to slip away to Vaniel.

CHAPTER 29
MOLLY

GETTING SITUATED IN VANIEL ISN'T EXACTLY SEXY, BUT ONCE WE get Alex seated on my bed and me in his lap, things get much hotter.

"Did you think of me today?" I ask breathlessly between kisses.

Alex's chest rumbles in a quiet laugh. "Ethan asked me if I was having a heart attack."

I pull back in confusion. "Why?"

"He thought I was having chest pains since I kept touching my pocket."

I laugh, and Alex leans forward to kiss me again. I'm straddling him, my knees pressing into the mattress on either side, which allows me to sit with Alex's hard cock right between my legs and grind on it. I purposefully wore a skirt for easy access, and the rough denim through my cotton panties provides just the right amount of pressure.

After a few minutes of making out, Alex pulls back. "Can anyone see us in here?"

The shades are down, and it's still light out, so no one can see in. However…

I bring my lips right to Alex's ear. "They can't see us. But they can hear us. The windows are open." If anyone is out there, the screens won't do much to muffle the noises. I think everyone's gone inside the big house, though.

Alex groans, and I stifle a laugh. If someone had told me weeks ago that Alex ran his mouth during sex, I wouldn't have believed them. Alex, during that first night, made my body clench around him and gave me wicked ideas with his dirty talk. Since then, things have escalated.

Usually, it's not a problem because we're alone at the house. Alex can make me scream, he can tell me what he wants to do to me, and with a little prompting, he can get real nasty.

"You'll just have to be quiet," I whisper, nipping his ear.

I extricate myself from his arms and reach up under my skirt to pull my panties off. Alex lifts his hips and opens his jeans, tugging them and his underwear down to mid-thigh.

He retrieves the condom from his pocket and rolls it on. When I approach, skirt around my waist, he grabs my hips and helps me settle on my knees, hovering over his cock. We both take sharp, drawn breaths as I position him at my entrance and lower myself to his lap.

I love the way Alex fills me. He lets go of my hips, leaning back to look at where we're joined. I place my hands on his chest and start to work my hips, but he stops me. Alex tugs my hand up to his mouth and, maintaining eye contact, sucks my first two fingers into his mouth. He drags them out slowly and then pushes them down between us.

"Make yourself come on my cock," he rasps.

I close my eyes and touch myself, rolling my clit between my saliva-slicked fingers. My other hand comes to rest on Alex's jean-clad knee behind me, allowing me to lean back.

"Fuck, I want to see that cunt come on my cock. It already feels so good." He's barely talking above a whisper. Almost like he's talking to himself instead of me, and I press harder against my clit, getting rough because I can feel the orgasm building inside me already. Occasionally, my fingers brush against the base of Alex's cock, and after a few strokes, I adjust so that my fingers are on either side of where he's seated, and my thumb takes over on my clit.

"You're so hot. Your pussy swallows me so good, doesn't it? Fucking made for me."

I squeeze my eyes tighter. My thumb works frantically, and combined with Alex's dirty mouth, I'm getting so close already. I squirm and shift, and when my orgasm overtakes me, my eyes fly open.

Alex's gaze meets mine and I can barely hear what he's saying over the roar in my ears.

"That's my good girl."

I shiver and Alex sits up, wrapping his arms around me and taking my mouth in a hot kiss. I'm boneless and satiated, so I follow him when he lays down. Alex's grip is tight, and he fucks me from beneath, his hips snapping up and his breath warm in my ear.

"I'm going to fuck you so good. Anything you want, I'll fucking give it to you. When we get home tonight—" *home,* my heart echoes, "—I'm going to make you come on my tongue over and—"

His words choke off as Alex pulses inside me.

After we clean up—body wipes for the win!—Alex and I head up to the big house. Ethan is grilling tonight, and Diane stands with him, chatting when we pass by. She's got long light brown hair and is about my height—so, short—and every time I see her, I have a hard time reconciling her beauty and fashionable clothes with someone I hear has been getting her hands dirty in the garden with Ethel.

Trixie's at the back door waiting for us, and Alex bends down to give her a good head scratch.

"I'm gonna set her bed up in the truck. I'll see you inside." Alex and Trixie lope off while I head into the kitchen.

As soon as I walk in, Colleen shoves a wine bottle at me and tells me to pour drinks. With Diane, our dinner party is now up to seven, and we go through a few bottles every Sunday. I run around taking drink orders and then set the wine glasses by Lia. She's slicing bread, even though she won't be able to eat it, and sways over to nudge my hip with hers. "You disappeared."

She laughs while I blush. "I don't think you have a leg to stand on," I tell her. "I'm pretty sure the first night I pulled in, you two were 'busy.'"

She shrugs and gets a far-off look. "Those Bedd men are pretty insatiable."

No argument there. "Wine tonight, or LaCroix?" I ask her.

"LaCroix."

"One effervescent beverage, coming right up!" I announce.

"Effervescent?" Ethan asks, coming in the door with Diane and Alex in tow, carrying platters of grilled veggies and meats. For some reason, he says it in a British accent.

"Effervescent!" Colleen shouts from the dining room where she's setting the table.

Ethan glances at Alex, who twirls his free hand and bows. "Effervescent."

I look at Lia, bewildered.

"Ignore them," she says. "It's a joke from when they were kids. They're making fun of fancy words."

Nerves take up residence inside my stomach. An inside joke. Sure, Dad and I have a bunch of them, but in a room full of Bedds, standing on the outside looking in, I feel like I've misstepped or maybe that *I'm* the joke.

I try to shake off my discomfort as we all take our seats and dig into the food. It's too loud to play my game with Ethel asking what she made, and she's deep in a chat with

Diane now about her heirloom tomatoes, so once we're done passing food, I turn to Lia and Ethan.

"How did the sales this weekend go?"

Lia beams. "Fantastic. Sold out of berries, of course, but I think Mootilda really made people linger afterward, and that helped sell everything else."

Besides Mootilda's debut, there was also a new vendor—a flower truck that sold bouquets and flower crowns—and the Feed 'n Seed store held a raffle for a riding lawn mower and split the proceeds with Bedd Fellows.

Ethan practically glows. "It was a great weekend. Every week we get more emails from potential vendors."

"It was a good day," Alex agrees.

Ethan gives his brother a rueful smile before looking down at his plate and cutting up his grilled chicken. "Just think; we could have been doing this all along if you hadn't left."

Beside me, Alex goes completely still. My eyes widen, and across the table, Lia's face drops.

"Left?" Alex's voice has dropped two octaves.

Ethan glances up, a frown tugging his lips down. "Yeah. I mean, I get it, Grandad wasn't listening to you. I just think of the time wasted when we could have been working the farm together."

"*Time wasted.*" The conversation at the other end of the table dies, and the screech of Alex's chair scraping back halts all the other noises until you could hear a pin drop as Alex glares down at his brother. "Just because I didn't spend my time running in circles while you and Grandad faffed around with your soybeans doesn't mean I *wasted my time.*"

"I didn't mean it like that," Ethan backtracks, rising to his feet and holding his hand out, placating. "Look, Grandad and I should have listened to you and Sam sooner. We could have used your help."

"So, it's my fault?"

"No." Ethan's fists clench at his sides. "Don't put words into my mouth. When you left—"

"I didn't leave!" Alex roars. Outside, Trixie barks, and Alex's face shutters, as if the noise reminds him he doesn't have to be here. His napkin lands on his uneaten food and he spins, knocking over the wooden chair as he stomps toward the door.

Ethan follows. "Now you're going to leave again? What, you still don't get how hard it was when you got a job at another farm?"

The five of us left at the table glance at each other, then scramble to our feet to follow. "Jesus, I hope they don't start wrestling," Colleen mutters. "They're too old for that."

My heart races faster than my feet, worried that Alex is already in pain and wrecked because how have none of us noticed?

Out in the yard, Alex strides toward his truck, where Trixie stands in the bed, barking at the commotion.

"I'm allowed to be upset at you!" Ethan shouts at his back. "I had twice as much work to do, and Grandad was pissy about it."

Alex reaches the truck and throws open the door.

"Alex." There's a warning in Ethan's voice.

Stopping to glare at his brother, Alex holds the door open while Trixie jumps out the truck bed and into the cab. Alex slides into the front seat.

"Goddamn it." Ethan takes his last two strides before the truck at a run and puts his hands on the tailgate, vaulting over to land in the bed of Alex's truck with a thump that makes the whole truck jostle.

Next to me, Lia squeaks. We've all gathered in the grass across the driveway to watch. Colleen's concern about wrestling seems unfounded since Alex just wants to get out of here. Ethel's face is drawn, and she clenches her hands into one fist at her breastbone. Lia covers her face with her hands.

"You okay?" I ask quietly while Alex starts his truck, and Ethan keeps yelling.

"Yeah, just totally inappropriately thinking about how hot it was that Ethan jumped into the truck like that. What is wrong with me?"

"ALEX!" Ethan bellows. Ethel walks up to the truck bed, and I can barely hear her placating tone over the rumble of the truck.

The door flies open again, and Alex steps out. His face is shockingly calm, and Ethan stills in the truck bed.

"Grandad wasn't pissy about it because it was his idea."

"What?" Ethan's voice rises with incredulity.

"Grandad told me to go. I didn't leave. He told me it was going to be your farm and we couldn't keep fighting over every little thing. So don't act like you made some enormous sacrifice when you ended up getting everything I ever wanted."

Alex's delivery is stony, too calm in Ethan's anger. In an instant, everything snaps and sizzles away like a drop of water on a hot frying pan. The two brothers stare at each other.

"Alex," I say gently, reaching out to touch his shoulder. He flinches as if he'd completely forgotten I was there, spinning to face me.

"Are you happy now?" he bites out. "You stuck your nose in our business. I hope you and Gran are satisfied with the way it all worked out."

I recoil, and behind me, Ethel gasps.

"It's your *family*, Alex," I whisper.

"And what do you know about family? You're here alone, Molly." He spreads his arms wide. "Easy to get along with them when you leave them behind, isn't it?"

I can't even answer, I just stare at him. This time, when Alex climbs into his truck, Ethan jumps off the bed and into the dirt. Alex peels out of the driveway and careens toward home.

CHAPTER 30
ALEX

I drive right past Udderly Creamy, barely even noticing the dark farm shop. A few minutes later I have to turn my headlights on, and the instinctual movement jolts me out of my head and makes me focus on what I'm doing.

I take a deep breath, attempting to relax my hold on the steering wheel, and shake my shoulders out. The truck is running west and I realize my body pointed me exactly where I wanted to go on autopilot: Here.

Sensing the mood shift, Trixie whines from the backseat and puts her paws on the armrest, bringing her head high enough to lick my ear. "Easy, girl," I say. "We're fine. We're going to be okay." I reach back and rub the scruff of her neck, my fingers running through her springy hair and feeling the rapid heartbeat underneath.

An hour or so later, I pull into Kit's parents' driveway. I don't even turn the truck off before the door opens and Kit strides out. He climbs into the passenger seat, greeting Trixie enthusiastically before buckling his seatbelt.

"Where to, buddy?" he asks me.

"Anywhere but Fork Lick," I say, sliding the truck into reverse and pulling out.

"I think the expression is supposed to be anywhere but

here, though that sounds like a diss on my hometown, so I'll let it slide."

There's a beat of quiet. "How did you know I was coming?"

"Molly called."

I glance at him over Trixie's head. She's standing on the center console, which I don't normally let her do, but she also knows I'm a sucker for her, especially when I'm in a bad mood.

"She's worried about you and gave me the rundown."

I don't say anything but turn onto Here's Main Street. Here used to be a tiny run-down town, but lately it's become a popular tourist destination—at least in the winter when skiers come to the old lodge. The summer's are quieter, and even though it's a beautiful mild June Sunday evening, it's dead downtown.

"What do you want? A drink? Some food? Sit outside?"

My stomach rumbles, and Trixie's tail whacks against the back of my seat. "All of the above."

"Deal." He points out the windshield. "See the string lights? Let's go there."

I park on the street and soon, we're seated at an outdoor table. Trixie is under our feet with her own doggie bowl, and one of the staff comes out to fist bump Kit, an Asian guy he introduces as Tuan.

He takes our order and Kit leans forward on his forearms. "Wanna talk about it?"

The drive cooled me off a bit, though I'm still pissed as hell at my brother.

Kit continues, knowing me well enough that silence is an answer in itself. "Ethan pressed your buttons, huh?"

"He acted like it was all my fault." The words tumble out. "It *wasn't my fault.*"

"I know."

"And my brother came to me, hat in hand, '*Oh Alex, look*

how good of a farmer you are. Teach me your ways,' the whole time thinking I'm to blame. Like, maybe he thought I should pay for something I didn't even do when we were kids."

"You were just a kid," Kit agrees.

"Exactly. I was fifteen. Grandad never listened to what I had to say."

"How old was Ethan?"

"Must've been sixteen or seventeen." I scrub my face in my hands. Ethan is sixteen months older than me. "And Gran. She had to have known. Why didn't she tell Ethan? Why does nobody talk to each other?" I spread my arms out wide, nearly knocking into a server carrying a stack of dirty plates, and apologize.

"Did she know?" Kit asks.

I keep my eyes and hands busy fiddling with a loose thread on the rolled-up napkin. Kit lets me gather my thoughts.

"I don't know for certain," I finally say. "Back then, maybe, I thought she would because they were essentially our parents, and Mom and Dad told each other everything. I didn't understand that it wouldn't be the same with Gran and Grandad. But now that we know he racked up all this debt without her knowing, and Gran's…well, she's a little different now."

"How so?"

It's hard to put my finger on what it is exactly, but I try to explain it. "You've been to the Sunday night dinners; you've seen her new garden. She invited Molly and Diane to live on the property."

"She's building her own little commune." Kit chuckles.

It hits me like a two-by-four, and I'm so stunned by the thought that I just blink and stare into space to absorb it.

Kit tilts his head.

"Gran's building a life after Grandad."

My best friend reaches over and squeezes my shoulder.

Our food comes, tofu banh mi for me and lemongrass stir-fry chicken for Kit. Tuan brings out a little bowl of plain chicken and rice for Trixie, who's going to be spoiled as hell tonight. I don't have any kibble for her, so I'm just hoping she won't develop a taste for the finer things in life.

"What about Molly?" Kit asks while cutting up his chicken.

Ugh. I don't want to talk about Molly. I can vividly recall the shock on her face when I snapped at her. She didn't know any better, but I did.

Molly didn't make me spend time with my family. I could have said no, could have ignored the phone calls and kept my life exactly the way it was.

But the allure of a house filled with my family, a life with people who love me instead of work for me tempted me too much.

One fight, and it's back to square one. Nothing between me and Ethan has changed, and even if I hadn't said a horrible thing to Molly, she's leaving me anyway. There's nothing I can do about it.

Kit interrupts my inward spiral. "You know I love you, right?"

Immediately, my insides unwind. I owe Molly a massive apology, after which she's going to leave me anyway, and Ethan will always view me as the villain, but I have Kit.

There's a nudge against my shin.

And Trixie.

CHAPTER 31
MOLLY

AFTER ALEX LEAVES, THE BEDDS HAVE A HEATED DISCUSSION IN the yard, and I'm on the outside looking in. Diane excuses herself, and I do, too, walking back to Vaniel in the dark. The Bedd family is probably regretting ever having met me.

Poor Alex. My heart aches for that teenage kid, who must have been so sweet and quiet, being told by the man who raised him to find somewhere else to go.

Why did I have to stick my nose into this family? Why? Didn't I learn my lesson after Oscar's family?

It was only hours ago that Alex was sitting on my bed, inside me.

I flop down on the bed, gazing up at the pictures on my ceiling. Those photos are supposed to remind me of fun times, to keep going, and share my adventures with my dad.

How come when I look up at them, I just feel so tired?

I haven't stayed the night in Vaniel in weeks.

I want to talk to someone, anyone, but I can't exactly go up to the big house and whine to any of the Bedd family— they've got their own problems and I'm probably not their favorite person right now. In the long run, I'm just a stranger passing through. Alex is family.

My book club is good for a laugh, but we don't talk about deep stuff.

Once again, I'm faced with the consequences of my own actions; by setting off on an adventure by myself, I've become more isolated.

Just like my dad when he has bad days.

I roll over on my bed and grab my phone. I will not give my dad all the details, but I need to talk to *someone*.

He answers on the third ring. "Hey, Molly-girl."

Oh no. Just hearing Dad's voice makes me go all watery. "Hi, Dad."

"Molly? What's wrong?"

I fight to hold back the tears, I really do, but as the seconds tick by, I realize it's a losing battle. "I screwed up, Dad."

"Molly? What happened?" Dad's voice is sharp, non-nonsense, tell-me-who-I-need-to-hurt. He might have gone a little soft now, but Officer Wesley Perkins is still a fighter…at least for me.

Dad listens while I tell him the whole story—leaving out the details about sleeping with Alex, obviously. But I leave enough in about Alex and Dad's no idiot. By the end, I have a pile of used tissues at my feet, and I'm a little worried I'm going to empty the box—I don't have a spare.

"He's an idiot," Dad says.

I laugh at his brashness.

"It's not funny," he continues. "The whole damn family are idiots. They don't deserve you."

"Thanks, Dad, for your completely unbiased opinion."

"You should leave. I'll send you some money so you can get back to your plans."

My plans include the Rock N Roll Hall of Fame, Yellowstone National Park, and the World's Only Corn Palace (let's face it, South Dakota doesn't have a lot going for it).

Money isn't really the problem. I don't know how to tell my dad, though. Even through Vaniel's dying batteries, Dad encouraged me to stay the course. I've just sunk thousands of dollars into my van, and I don't want to disappoint my dad by not finishing the trip.

The one I'm doing *for him*.

I've been quiet for too long.

"Oh, Molly-girl." Dad sighs. "This is supposed to be fun."

I know. I wasn't supposed to get my heart broken. The words can't make it past my throat, though.

"Do you want to come home?"

I nod, and then remember he can't see me, and whisper, "Yes."

"Then come home. I miss you."

I bike to Udderly Farm early in the morning, bracing myself to have a talk with Alex on his breakfast break, but when I park my bike at the farm shop and walk up the hill, I don't see Alex's truck. Curious, I step inside the house, kick my flip-flops off, and come into the kitchen. Jesús, Anna, and Perry are at the table staring at me. No Alex. No Trixie. Everyone looks at me with concern. I guess word's gotten around about what happened.

"Hi." I give them a half-smile. "Is Alex here?"

"No," Jesús says. "He stayed with Kit last night."

"Come, eat." Anna gestures.

As always, it smells fantastic, but being in Alex's house is uncomfortable. I'm unsure when he'll come back and how upset he'll be with me, and I would rather just get out of here.

Get home.

I shove my hands in the pockets of my shorts. "I'm actually leaving. If you need me to, I can work at the farm shop today, but..."

"It's fine," Perry says. "We'll take care of it."

"Okay. Thanks." Awkwardly, I walk back to Alex's room

and pick up the few things of mine in there—my gloves, my ointment, a phone charger. It all gets bundled into my bag.

I cut through the hallway instead of going back through the kitchen to leave, but Anna calls after me. Wordlessly, she wraps me in a hug, and I fight back tears.

"You're going to be okay," is all she says, and then lets go.

I bike back to Bedd Fellows and have pretty much the same conversation with Ethel and Ethan. This time, though, the mutual guilt hanging in the air is oppressive.

"Are you sure, dear?" Ethel asks. "You know you're welcome to stay, right?"

"Yeah," I assure her. "I know. But Vaniel is ready to go, and so am I."

I don't tell them I'm heading straight home. I'd rather let them think that it's just time to move on. After all, my feelings about Alex don't matter in the long run. I'm just a woman who's passing through. They're Alex's *family*.

Here's a wonder of van life: I grab a few things from the pole barn, and I'm ready to go. It's been two hours since I woke up this morning, and I've cut all ties to the Bedd family.

I start Vaniel.

Baabara is the only one that watches me leave.

CHAPTER 32
ALEX

YOU CAN TAKE THE MAN OUT OF THE DAIRY FARM, BUT YOU CAN'T take the dairy farm out of the man. I wake up before sunrise in the guest bedroom of Kit's parents' house. The Hutchinsons have always been kind to me and treated me like family, even though I'm just one of Kit's many, many friends.

I check in with Perry, who says everything is fine and to take my time getting back. When I get there this afternoon, I'll send both him and Jesús home as a thank you for doing the morning chores without me.

I can count on one hand the number of times that I haven't woken up at Udderly since I moved in.

There are missed calls from my family—literally everyone, even Jackson and Samuel, who I haven't seen in months—but nothing from Molly. I ignore my family and instead slip out of the Hutchinsons' house. I grab an old leash out of my truck, worried about local laws and stranger danger with other dogs, and walk toward Main Street, Trixie at my heel.

It's not close, but it's still walkable. The fresh air and movement will do me good, and I take the time to think about apologizing to Molly. Yes, my family hurt me, but that's nothing new, and it's not her fault.

I find a coffeehouse, a place that reminds me of our renovated farm shop—a little kitschy for my taste, but most people would say I have no sense of style when it comes to decor. I order a black coffee and a pup cup and survey my reading options. There are local magazines and guidebooks, a testament to the tourism industry. I pick up a few things and take them out to the bench where Trixie waits. She shoves her snout into the paper cup and goes to town.

It's hard to focus on the reading. I'm only halfway through an article on the family that owns the local ski resort when Kit flops down on the bench beside me.

And when I say flop, I mean *full-body flop*. His head ends up on my thigh, and he closes his eyes and pretends to snore. Trixie gets up to sniff his face before he pushes her away.

"You didn't have to get up," I tell him.

He ignores me. I go back to my article, and Trixie shoves her nose deeper into the paper cup.

I have to make sure my family apologizes to Molly, too. Maybe I need to get Ethan to agree that we don't share an employee again. It shouldn't be difficult—even though it's a small town, Ethan doesn't really have hired help. Our family has always been enough to support the farm, even now that it's diversifying.

I'm not a big enough idiot to suggest that Molly quits one of her jobs. But maybe I could have her move Vaniel to Udderly so that she doesn't need her deal with Gran.

Hell, maybe she doesn't even need Vaniel.

No wait. This is one-hundred percent fantasy, because no matter what I do, Molly's still leaving at the end of the summer.

Fuck. Here I am, fantasizing about Molly staying with me when I know she's gotta finish her trip and get home to her dad. She's still got months of travel ahead of her in that van. She'll probably be glad to leave all this drama behind.

"You might as well put the magazine down. You aren't fooling anyone."

I put the magazine down…on Kit's face. He sputters and gets up, throwing the magazine at my chest and ambling inside the shop. He returns with a plate full of pastries and a mug of light brown, doctored coffee.

"You gonna drive back to Fork Lick today?"

"Yup."

"Apologize your ass off to Molly?"

"Yup."

"Talk to your family?"

"Maybe."

Kit nods. "Acceptable plan. Your family can wait till tomorrow."

Hours later, I pull into the farm shop parking lot and climb out of my truck. I let Trixie loose with a "go long," and she dashes off to the field. The chicken coop is in the near one today, and Trixie does a wide lap around it, mindful of the hens.

I open the door to the farm shop and freeze. Imara, not Molly, is at the counter. She waves. "Hi, Mr. Bedd."

There's a rock settling in my gut. "Where's Molly?" It comes out sharp and harsh, and I wince.

"Um, I don't know. Perry said I should talk to you about my schedule for the rest of the week?"

Oh shit. I back out of the shop without answering and whistle for Trixie, who comes barreling toward me. She doesn't even slow down as I hold the door open for her, and she leaps into the cab. There's still a bug up her butt, and she does a lap inside, bouncing from the front seat to the back seat and back before I get the truck started and roll out of the parking lot.

Molly wouldn't be waiting for me at my house. She'd be in the farm shop or…

The rock sinks further as I put the pedal to the metal to get to Bedd Fellows. I try calling Molly, but she doesn't answer. Trixie whines and nudges me.

My stomach completely bottoms out when I drive around the back of the farmhouse and see that Vaniel's gone. The rock just disappears, leaving me with a hollow, gutted feeling.

I've fucked up so badly.

A door slams, and I look to my right. Through the swirl of road dust I've kicked up, I can see Gran on the back porch, her hands on her hips.

I roll the window down. Trixie sticks her head out and gives Gran a joyful bark. "Where's Molly?"

"She left this morning. Can you come in to talk?"

I squeeze my eyes shut, thinking. Molly would head to Pennsylvania, probably, on the thruway. "What time did she leave? Do you know where she went?"

When I open my eyes, Gran is right next to my truck. She gives Trixie an absent-minded pat on the head. "She left about an hour ago, and I don't know exactly where she's going." Gran hesitates. "I really want to talk to you, honey, and so does Ethan. But if you need to go after Molly, we'll wait."

I grip the steering wheel and try to think. Where would she be going? It could literally be anywhere.

"Maybe her dad could help you?" Gran suggests.

I have his number on her emergency contact sheet. I nod, and Gran pats the doorframe. "We'll be here when you're ready."

I drive back to Udderly and find Molly's paperwork in my office. I dial the number for her dad, Wesley Perkins.

A grumpy voice answers. "If you're a telemarketer, I'm going to shove my boot so far up your ass—"

Belatedly, I realize it's a little before six a.m. in Washington.

"Mr. Perkins? This is Alex Bedd. I'm Molly's...boss."

"Her boss, huh? So, I suppose this is a business call about how you slept with my daughter?"

I swallow. I did not think this through very well. "No, sir."

"No, you didn't sleep with my daughter?" He barks.

Jesus. "No, sir. I mean…I, uh…That's not why I'm…" Oh, fuck it. "Do you know where Molly is?"

"Yes."

"She's safe?"

His voice softens a fraction of an inch, and I'll take it. "Yes."

"Is there any chance," I close my eyes, "that you would tell me where I could find her so I can apologize to her? I'll fly wherever it takes."

There's silence on the line for so long I think he might not answer.

"You fucked up, son."

I exhale, partly in relief and partly in surprise at him calling me "son." It's stupid, and I know he doesn't mean anything by it, but no one's called me son in years. "I know. My whole family did."

"So why should I tell you where she is?"

I pinch the bridge of my nose, standing in my office trying to figure out how to explain to Molly's dad how much she means to me. Memories resurface of the past two months; Molly's excitement at everything, the way she teased me, the way she made my life richer, less lonely. Not just with her presence but with her gravitational pull that sucked everyone in—my family, Kit, my farm hands, even my dog.

I take a deep breath and confess. "Sir, I'm in love with your daughter. I don't know if she'll forgive me, and I have no idea how we could stay together, but she deserves to hear my apology. I can't stand the thought of her time with us being stained by the stupid thing I said. She's amazing, and her trip is worth more than my pride—and yours."

A big sigh comes through the phone. "Fine. Fly to

Spokane and I'll pick you up from the airport. If you can make it today, maybe you can talk to her."

"She's not going to Pennsylvania?"

"No." I almost hear the *dumbass* tacked on at the end of the word. "She's driving home, only stopping to sleep."

"But, that's going to take her..." It's got to be at least a three-day trip.

"You come *today*," he growls, "and *maybe* I'll let you talk to her. After you and I have a chat."

"Yes, sir."

CHAPTER 33
MOLLY

SEEING MY DAD'S TRAILER FOR THE FIRST TIME IN EIGHT MONTHS is like a fresh breeze hitting my face.

Or maybe it's because I've driven Vaniel for three days straight to get home, and the air inside is stale.

Either way, I park my van right out front next to Dad's sedan, and before the engine's even off, the door flies open, and Dad steps out. I have never felt more like a daddy's girl than I do launching myself into his arms.

"Hey Molly-girl."

I thought I'd been all cried out—after getting yelled at by my boss and unofficial boyfriend and then giving up on my dad's dream—but shockingly, tears form in my eyes again. If I cry, I'll end up with a major headache again, and I'm so sick of being sad and lonely. I pull away slightly so Dad shifts his grip to my shoulders and guides me toward Vaniel.

"How about you give me the grand tour?"

We spend at least an hour poring over Vaniel. I show Dad every nook and cranny and he asks tons of questions. So many questions.

"We could take him for a spin around the block?" Dad suggests. "Driver up to Hooligans for some ice cream?"

I laugh. "I just drove, like, forty hours. Can we not? We can do it tomorrow, I promise."

"Fine," Dad grumbles, but it's good-natured.

Arm around me again, we walk up the steps to the trailer.

"Are you missing New York?" he asks me.

I don't even have to think about it. "Yeah." I miss the scenery in the Catskills, I miss Ethel and Trixie and the stupid adorable goats, and, mostly, I miss Alex. My heart aches for him still, and here, walking side by side with my dad, I think about how lucky I am to have a simple, straightforward family.

"Well, let's see how badly you miss it," Dad says, and before I can ask him what he means, he opens the door to his home and steps inside the living room...where Alex sits on the couch.

Alex rises to his feet and whacks his head on the cabinets above the couch. "Ouch, shit."

"Language," Dad reprimands, sitting down on the opposite corner of the couch from where Alex was sitting.

"Language?" I sputter, because that's what my mind focuses on instead of the massive man in front of me. "You don't care about cursing."

"It's his way of punishing me," Alex says, the corner of his mouth twitching up in amusement. "One of the ways he's punishing me," he corrects. Alex steps away from the recessed couch where he can stand up straight.

Dad pulls out his reading glasses and picks up his tablet from the table. He looks pointedly at me. "I'll be right here, and Alex and I have an agreement: if you want him to get lost, I'll kick his ass out of here so fast his grandma will hear the sonic boom. Isn't that right, son?"

"Yes, sir."

My mind is officially blown. What is happening here? I have so many questions.

I start with an easy one and fold my arms across my chest. "How long have you been here?"

"Two days."

"What about the farm?"

"Perry and Jesús are doing just fine with the part-timers."

"Trixie?"

"Staying with Ethan."

"Ethel?"

Alex looks at me, exasperated. "Molly, everyone's fine. Can we talk about us now?"

I set my jaw. "When I left, everyone was not fine. You and Ethan were so mad at each other."

His face shifts to guilt. "I know. And I put you in the crossfire, and I am so sorry about that. None of it was your fault, and I've—apparently—been harboring a lot of angry feelings with Grandad and Ethan over the past fifteen years."

Alex shifts closer. "Molly, I never should have put you in the middle of that argument. It was a disagreement fifteen years in the making, one that was fueled by lingering feelings of abandonment and grief." His eyes flicker over to my dad, who's pretending to read. "Mr. Perkins and I have been discussing it a lot, and he suggested I talk to a therapist about it. I have an appointment in Albany next week."

Relief flows through me, and those stupid tears resurface and spill over my cheeks. "I'm glad you're going to take care of yourself."

Movement out of the corner of my eye catches my attention, and Dad holds a tissue box toward me. I take one and wipe my eyes. When I look back up, Alex holds my gaze, the deep copper of his eyes dripping with sincerity. "I am so sorry, Molly."

"Thank you," I whisper. "Forgiven."

Alex's hands twitch by his side. I close the gap between us and wrap my arms around his solid waist. Alex's whole body relaxes against me, and even if he's been in Spokane for two days, he still smells like a New York summer in the barn—hay (or maybe barley), sunshine, sweet milk, and the warmth of animals.

I bury my face in Alex's flannel. The apology was perfect, but I sit here, wrapped up in Alex, and my tears fall even harder. There's nowhere to go from here. Alex is going to get on a plane and head home to his farm, see a therapist, and maybe patch things up with Ethan.

Thousands of miles away.

I pull back, and Dad gives me another tissue, which I use to blow my nose and wipe my face. "I can't believe you flew all the way over here and stayed two days with my dad just to apologize."

Alex rubs the back of his neck. "Well, I stayed in a hotel room. And I didn't exactly come just to apologize."

"What do you mean?"

Alex straightens and runs a hand down his beard. "I thought, maybe, I could take you out on a proper date."

"A proper date?" I echo. "Um…why?" Of all the things Alex could have said, I wasn't expecting this. It's one thing to ask for my forgiveness; it's another to want to keep me around.

Alex holds my gaze. "Because I'm crazy about you, Molly. The two months you've been in my life have been the best I've ever had. And I don't want to let you go."

"But…I live here."

"We, uh, have some thoughts about that."

"We?"

"Yeah. Your dad and I." Alex gestures to my dad, who's no longer pretending to read. "I think you should finish your road trip."

My eyes dart to my dad.

"Actually," Dad adds. "I want *us* to finish your road trip and move to New York, if you want."

"I...what? You didn't want to go with me before."

Dad sighs. "Molly, you're young and—" Dad gestures to his body, where his pants hide his prosthetic, and I know the gesture encompasses so much more than a missing leg. "—more physically and emotionally capable than I am. I wanted you to have fun, and I didn't want to hold you back. It seems like you *did* have fun, maybe too much—" he side-eyes Alex "—but if you want to drive back to New York, I want to come with you. We can finish the list, and I can see some of those cute goats you've told me so much about in person."

"Or," Alex adds quickly. "There are dairy farms here, and I can find a new position. It'll take me some time, maybe six months, to make sure Udderly's in good hands, but I can find work."

I shake my head, immediately rejecting the thought. Alex's whole life is in Fork Lick, and even while it might be a lonely one sometimes, it doesn't have to be. Even I, an only child with one parent and a knowledge gap about big families, can see that Alex's life is rich. And while Trixie can come with him, he'd lose his friendship with Kit and the potential to repair his relationship with his family.

"You'd lose a lot of things that you love," I tell him.

Alex steps forward, cupping my face with his hands. "I love *you*, Molly."

Damnit. I'm crying again. "I love you, too." My gentle man bends down and plants a soft kiss on my lips. I push up on my toes and wrap my arms around his neck to pull him down for more. Alex steps even closer, putting our bodies flush and wrapping his arms around me.

Until Dad clears his throat, and we pull apart. My cheeks go up in flames. I've never kissed anyone in front of my dad.

"So, are we moving to New York?" Dad asks.

"Yes," I say. "Yes!"

Alex's smile is the widest I've ever seen it.

A thought occurs to me. "Wait. Where is Dad going to live?"

Alex clears his throat. "Actually, I have some thoughts about that."

CHAPTER 34
ALEX

I STAY TWO MORE DAYS IN SPOKANE. MR. PERKINS CONSIDERABLY warms up to me now that Molly and I are back together. The two days I waited for Molly, he had me help him with projects around his trailer. I wonder if, even then, he was thinking about selling it so that he could move.

Molly and I go on a proper date, then back to my hotel room before I drop her off at their home, and Mr. Perkins and I both pretend I haven't just had sex with his daughter. I help them buy a tent and air mattress for someone to sleep on while they drive Vaniel back to New York, and Mr. Perkins invites me to play pickleball with him and his VA buddies.

It's an embarrassing loss because I've never heard of pickleball before, and being a dairy farmer doesn't require much hand-eye coordination. I make a note, though, to look into veterans' services in the Catskills and put together a mental Rolodex of people his age in Fork Lick who might make good friends for him.

Molly takes me to the airport. I give her a tight hug at the curb and we both linger as long as we can. I'm nervous about leaving. What if they get to Fork Lick and decide not to stay?

What if they don't even make it back to Fork Lick? Or Molly and Mr. Perkins cancel the drive? What if they turn around once they check Pennsylvania off the list, and I never see Molly again?

"This doesn't feel real," she says. "Like I'm going to wake up in our trailer and I'll have dreamed the entire last eight months. How has so much happened?"

I rub my hands up and down her arms. "Same," I tell her. "But if I wake up, it will have been a fantastic dream." I allow a small smile. "And then I'll come find you."

That's what I would do. If Molly turns around, I'll come find her again.

Her smile lights up. Maybe sometimes Molly needs me to be the optimistic one, and that I can do.

With one last kiss, I pick up my bag and wave goodbye to the perky love of my life.

By the time I pull my truck into Bedd Fellows Farm, it's early evening. I text my brother to let him know I'm on my way to retrieve Trixie.

This trip was the first time I'd spent so many nights away from Udderly, but also the longest I've ever been away from Trixie since I adopted her. I hope she doesn't think I abandoned her.

The moment my truck pulls up Trixie flies out of Baabara's palace. I bend a knee, and she launches herself at me, licking my face and wiggling so hard I have to put her down. There's too much energy contained in one small body, and Trixie runs laps around me, around the yard, up the stairs to the house, and back down to my arms again.

Jesus, you would think I was returning from an overseas deployment or something. Finally, her energy gets pushed down to just her tail, and she flops over onto her back, tongue lolling and jowls succumbing to gravity. I put my hand on her chest, feeling that soft, baby-fine fur and her racing heart.

"She isn't the only one who missed you," Gran calls down from the top of the stairs.

I keep my focus on Trixie so Gran doesn't see my reaction. She comes down the stairs and places her hand on my shoulder. "Stay for dinner. Let's talk."

I give Trixie a final pat and she races back to Baabara. "Thanks for taking care of her, Gran."

"She's my only grand baby." Gran sniffs while we walk back to the dining room. "She's been sitting on the porch with me every day. You always leave her out in the truck."

"She *likes* the truck. She also really likes Baabara's shed."

Gran gives me side-eye. "Molly told me about her fancy dog bed."

"It's a *dog bed*," I argue.

Loud voices come from the kitchen before Ethan and Colleen step out, carrying platters of sandwich fixings. Four place settings are on the table.

"Where's Lia?" I ask. "Or that seed woman…"

"*Diane*," Gran says with a glare, "is no longer here. I'd hoped she'd stay for at least another week, but she left Monday. I think she was uncomfortable after the fight. Lia is having dinner with her brother."

Chastened, I sit down, and we make our sandwiches. There's lunch meat and veggies, but Gran hands me a bowl of egg salad.

Ethan asks me about Spokane, and everyone listens while I tell them about Molly's dad and that they'll be driving back to Fork Lick, but it'll take a while. Colleen has been running the summer reading program at the Fork Lick Library and Ethan and Gran are busy freezing, preserving, and making syrup out of blueberries.

When we've polished off the sandwiches, Gran laces her fingers together and gazes at me from across the table. My palms start to sweat. I don't want to fight with Ethan or Gran again.

"I didn't know what my Eugene said to you until it was too late, and I only got his side of the story. It was a long time ago, but would you be willing to tell us about it?"

Uncomfortable memories push inside my brain, and I shift in my chair. I glance at Ethan, who flashes a smile at me.

"Grandad was pretty stubborn," he says.

I blow out a breath. "Yeah, he was. I don't even remember what we were fighting about, you and me."

"We fought about a lot." His smile is gone now.

I shift forward, pushing my plate away so that I can rest my forearms on the table. "I know you didn't expect to raise us," I say, eyes on my plate. "And it must have been hard to be saddled with five kids when you were supposed to be thinking about retirement."

A gentle hand touches my arm. I look up at Gran. "You don't have to justify our behavior."

Colleen, beside me, puts a hand on my shoulder.

I swallow. "I don't remember what his exact words were, but he said that this was going to be Ethan's farm someday, and he couldn't have me arguing with the two of them all the time. He asked what my plans were after I graduated high school, and when I told him I was going to work the farm, just like he did, and Dad did, and Ethan was going to do, Grandad said I should think about doing something else.

"So, I did." I shrug.

Across from me, Ethan's jaw is tense. "He was so mad when you got the job at Udderly, though. I don't understand that."

I remember that, too. At the time, it felt like I just couldn't win either way.

"Your grandfather was a proud man," Gran says. "But he had a lot of stress on his plate and, while I'm not trying to justify his behavior and he wouldn't say it outright, he worried he was failing you kids all the time."

"But that's in the past now," Ethan adds.

I frown. It is, and it isn't. The way we grew up is coloring how we see each other now. I have old wounds from my childhood, and I bet Ethan does, too.

"And I owe you an apology for how I acted more recently."

"You didn't know," I say.

"I know you're my brother," he tells me, "and I haven't always been the best at communicating. But I'd like to get better. And I really like spending time with you–and not just working together." He punches me in the shoulder playfully. "It's good having you around more often. Let's make a habit of it?"

"Okay," I say.

Colleen lifts her glass of lemonade, which is mostly empty. "To family," she says. "Both original *and* new additions are always welcome."

CHAPTER 35
MOLLY

For the first time, Vaniel turns up the drive to Udderly Creamy Farm. Dad sits in the passenger side, gazing out the window, and I'm hit with a sense of renewed appreciation for the beauty of Alex's farm.

"That's the farm shop," I point out. Imara and a former employee who is now a college student home for the summer have been working in the shop. Once school starts again, I'll be working during the week. I'm only working for one Bedd brother this time.

The pasture next to it is empty since it's almost seven, and the animals must be up at the barn. "That's where I fell in cow shit," I add, pointing to the grassy hill as Vaniel climbs the steep driveway.

"It's beautiful here. Summer is so green."

I smile. It is. And I can't believe that I'll be living here now. I'll get to see New York through all the seasons.

Dad and I spent three weeks driving back to Fork Lick. We made memories together, visiting roadside attractions and national parks. In an odd turn of events, I was sending pictures of my adventure to Alex instead of Dad. Every night, I'd talk to him and tell him about my day, and we'd count down the miles together until I'd see him again.

We reach the top of the hill, and I park next to Alex's truck. Trixie races out of the barn to greet us. She barks until I exit the van and come around the front. Then she recognizes me, and it's all butt waggles and yipping and bouncing around until she gets herself back under control.

Then she gives Dad a good sniffing, spending extra time on his prosthetic, which is visible since Dad's wearing shorts today. It's the beginning of August, and it was the hottest day of the year so far, so we were thankful to be driving in Vaniel's air-conditioned comfort since we left the Allegheny National Forest right after lunch.

With Dad, we've done more camping-style overnights than boondocking in parking lots or on public property. Surprisingly, Dad has enjoyed sleeping in the tent. He calls it communing with nature—which is also what he says when he's peeing in the woods—so all around, Dad's getting a lot of one-on-one time with the outdoors.

"Molly." The deep voice full of affection draws my attention away from Trixie and toward the big man striding over from the barn. I take off at a run and launch myself at Alex. He catches me, lifting me up so I'm even with his face and giving me a panty-melting, completely-inappropriate-in-front-of-my-dad kiss.

"I missed you," I say when I pull away.

"I missed you, too."

He sets me down and greets my dad with a handshake. I stick myself to Alex's side and twine my fingers through his.

"Alex, good to see you," Dad says. "Did it come in?"

My boyfriend grins. "It did."

"Did what come in?" I ask.

The two men exchange a glance.

"Wait, have you been cahooting?" I put my hands on my hips. I knew the two of them were talking, but mostly I thought that was logistics planning. Dad's going to stay here for a few weeks, living in Vaniel while I'm in the house with

Alex. He's going to think about whether he wants to move to Fork Lick permanently and sell the trailer when he goes back to Spokane. And Dad and Alex have been talking about things he can do to help around the farm.

"Me? Cahooting?" Alex feigns innocence, while my dad just grins.

I mock-scowl at Alex, who holds out a hand, beckoning me to follow him. "Come here. I have a surprise."

Dad starts toward the house like he knows where he's going, and I ignore Alex's hand. Instead, I slide my arm around his waist while his comes to rest on my shoulders. A kiss lands on the top of my head.

"How's your family?" I ask.

"Good," he says. Alex told me about his conversation with Ethel and his siblings. Although I don't ask about his therapy sessions, he often calls me afterward, trying to decompress emotionally. My heart gets wrung out for him every time. "You'll see them all tomorrow," he says.

Today is Friday, so tomorrow, I'll be bringing Dad to the berry picking. Raspberries are in season now, so there's even more ground to cover. Alex is bringing one of the calves again —not Mootlida, she's aged out—and, of course, the flavored milk.

And then, of course, there's dinner on Sunday. I've been keeping up with Ethel, watching some of her videos she's been posting with the help of Diane, who has returned to Bedd Fellows. Ethel told me Sam, Colleen's twin, is coming to dinner this Sunday too.

Ethel also told me she and Ethan went on a scavenger hunt around the house for two days, trying to find where Ethel stored the leaves for the dining room table so they could expand it and fit everyone.

Instead of leading us into the house, Alex goes around the backside. I've never been this way and had assumed it was just a small yard that butts up against the woods, but when we turn the corner, it's not an empty yard.

There's a boxcar—an honest to god boxcar—sitting in Alex's backyard.

"What....?" Alex's arm slides off my shoulders as I step ahead of him. "What is...? No! You didn't!"

Alex laughs. The boxcar is red—red! Just like in the story! —and rests on its wheels in the grass. It's got black trim, and while the paint is not in good shape, the walls are solid and thick.

I place my hands on the side. It's warm from the sun, and the wheels mean that it's set up pretty high.

"What is this doing here?" I ask, awe softening my voice.

"I thought maybe you'd like to fix it up. It's kind of impractical to travel in it, but it could be an office or a, uh..." Alex rubs the back of his neck and pointedly *does not* look at my dad. "...in-law's suite. Someday. Maybe."

"Oh my god. Can we get in? Does it open?"

Alex helps me slide the heavy doors back and then climb up onto the floor. It's a big step up, and we have to give Dad a hand, but soon we're all standing in the long, empty space— even Trixie, whose nose huffs in the corner.

I gawk and run my hands along the walls. The ceiling is curved, and the sides are wood paneling that's seen better days. It's stiflingly hot, but I don't care.

I turn to Dad. "Did you have anything to do with this?"

Dad shakes his head. "It was all Alex's idea."

I fling myself at Alex again, wrapping him in an enormous hug. "Thank you so much. This is going to be amazing."

He pulls away just enough to gaze at me, a soft smile on his lips. "I can't wait to see what you come up with."

Much later, after we eat dinner and Dad goes to bed in the guest room, Alex and I lay in a sweaty pile on his bed. Alex had to literally bite his knuckles to keep quiet, and I think we did an okay job. Trixie certainly slept through it—she's snoring in her fancy-ass dog bed.

After a few minutes, Alex turns to me. "Are you thinking about your boxcar?"

"Oh my god, yes." I cover my face with my hands. "Sorry."

The bed bounces while he laughs. "I'm glad you're excited. And I'm glad I get to have a front-row seat to watch you do this."

I turn to him in the dark and whisper. "Thank you for the new adventure."

He whispers back. "Thank you for being my adventure."

Want to find out what's next for Bedd Fellows Farm? Book three is For Fork's Sake by Karen Grey, where nerdy soil scientist Sam finds passionate, idealist Diane interviewing his grandma for her YouTube channel. Feathers fly between these farm business rivals!

Want more Alex and Molly? Newsletter subscribers get an exclusive epilogue of their adventures. Subscribe to read about a big party.

FARM 2 FORKING SERIES

Bedd Fellows Farm is in trouble. Grandad bequeathed the five Bedd siblings a heap of debt, along with a troublesome sheep, and they're all too stubborn to accept the help they need to dig their way out of the compost pile.

Join authors Lainey Davis, Liz Alden, Karen Grey, Erin Mallon, and Ember Leigh as they share un-baa-lievable tales of love, laughter, and sexy shenanigans, all set in the bucolic fictional town of Fork Lick, New York.

Meddling grandmas, nosy neighbors, and boinking abound in these steamy romantic comedies.

Since You've Bean Gone by Lainey Davis
Butter You Up by Liz Alden
For Fork's Sake by Karen Grey
Bringing Home the Bacon by Erin Mallon
A Fork in the Road by Ember Leigh

MORE FROM THE AUTHORS

Catch up with the Bedds' neighbors in the Planted and Plowed series by Lainey Davis. Asher Thorne is the hero of Sappy Go Lucky.

Take your romcoms with a side of wanderlust. Kit gets his own story in the upcoming Anywhere But Here series by Liz Alden. In the meantime, check out Aged Like Fine Wine, where four best friends explore Europe and love after forty!

Stayed tuned for a new small town romcom series coming soon from Karen Grey, set down the road from Fork Lick and kicking off with single dad Ben's story! In the meantime, check out her nostalgic romance at karengrey.com.

As a girl with four brothers, Colleen Bedd knows what it's like to be "one of the guys." For more strong heroines who aren't afraid to go head-to-head with their fellas, dive into The Natural History Series by Erin Mallon.

Jackson's leading lady hails from Bayshore, a small, lakeside Ohio town that sets the stage for Ember's other rom-coms.

Visit Bayshore now to meet the Daly brothers, and to get ready for the next series launching soon.

ACKNOWLEDGMENTS

This was a joyous book to write, mostly because of my fabulous co-collaborators. Creating the Bedd family with them has been so much fun, and I greatly appreciate getting to spread my wings into small town romance with them.

Thanks to Kristin Hanes for her help consulting all things vanlife and translating my ideas from sailboat to van.

Thank you as well to Sara Whitney and Elise Kennedy for beta reading.

And as always, a big thank you to my husband, who encouraged me so much from day one, and my parents, all five of them, who supported this book in one way or another.

www.ingramcontent.com/pod-product-compliance
Lightning Source LLC
Chambersburg PA
CBHW032225190726

48289CB00007BA/2387